# Her Mother's Bible

by

*Isabella Alden*

*1890*

This book has been edited in order to update certain points of spelling, grammar, and punctuation usage. All of the reprints in our Keepers of the Faith Collection are taken from the works of authors who display the desire, above all, to strengthen the reader's Christian walk. However, any good, moral author can still have an occasional view that is less than healthy, especially for young people. Or, he or she might, while churning out a work, add something to enhance the story that, with time for second thoughts, might have been left out or revised.

As it has always been our policy not to offer books to the public that we feel could not be offered to the Saviour, Himself, all of our reprints are proofread by several individuals, and have been revised and amended to offer the purest and most wholesome reading experience possible from the author's work.

# CHAPTER I.

*Incline my heart unto thy testimonies and not to*
*covetousness.*
*Trust in the Lord and do good; so shalt thou dwell*
*in the land, and verily thou shalt be fed.*
*Bear ye one another's burdens and so fulfill the law*
*of Christ .*
*The Lord our God will we serve, and His voice will*
*we obey.*

"Yes," said Mrs. Selmser, fingering the leaves of the
large old Bible with loving touch, "it is all I got; no, I
wasn't disappointed, because I didn't expect anything.
Maria was the youngest child, and Mother has lived with
her so many years it stood to reason that she would leave
everything to her. To be sure, as Reuben says, Maria has
enough, and more than enough, while we find it pretty
hard work to make the two ends meet; but then, Mother
didn't sense that; she was old, you see, and didn't think
much about money matters, anyhow; and she had no
great sum to leave, I suppose; she has always paid her
way at Maria's. Those children were great pets of hers,
of course, being with them ever since they were born; she
didn't know our children much. Mother wasn't able to
travel for a number of years before she died, and we
could never afford to take the children to see her; so it

was all natural enough, and I'm not a mite disappointed, though I can see that Reuben is, just a little; that's natural, too. But I've got the old Bible, and I'd rather have it this minute than anything Mother had to leave. You see it is the one she used regularly for years and years, and it is all marked up with her verses. You can hardly turn a page but you will come across a verse marked in red ink, or blue ink, or green ink; Mother was a great hand to mark her Bible, and so was Father. It makes the verses kind of stand out, you know, so you are obliged to think about them, even if you are in a hurry; and it kind of seems to help you get the sense of them; I don't know why, I'm sure; Maria didn't think so. She never liked to see a Bible marked up; she said it didn't look neat.

"I suppose that was why Mother gave the message to me that she did. Said she, 'Jane, I'm going to leave my big old Bible to you and your children; I have a feeling that it will help you more that it will Maria or John.' Some way it did me good to have Mother say that, and know that she had thought about it and planned to leave her Bible to us; and I'm right glad to get hold of it. I tell the children I hope they will learn every one of the marked verses this year, and store them up; for their grandmother never marked verses at random, as you may say; she picked them out to live by."

All the while she talked, Mrs. Selmser kept up that tender little almost caressing touch of the worn Bible, and as she turned its leaves and one caught glimpses of the marked verses, it gave the impression that the Grandmother had lived on a great many.

"Yes," said Mrs. Selmser, smiling fondly, when her attention was called to this, "my boy Ralph says, 'Why, Mother, if we undertake to learn all of Grandmother's verses, we might as well learn the whole Bible and be done with it.' And I tell them I don't know as they could learn anything that would make them wiser."

Miss Edwards, her caller, reached for the Bible and turned the leaves with careful fingers and paused over some of the marked verses with interested face.

"Trust in the Lord and do good; so shalt thou dwell in the land and verily thou shalt be fed," read Miss Edwards. "That is heavily marked."

"Yes; and I make no doubt there was a story belonging to it if only I knew it. If you look close you will see Father's initials in the corner, and the letters T.P. made very small. You know about the old lady who marked her Bible all over with T.P.'s, don't you? Why, she meant tried and proved. That story made a great impression on Father, I know, and he used to mark some verses that way; so did Mother. I know some of the stories. I only wish I knew all of them."   "I only wish they would come true to us, as well as to Grandfather and Grandmother," said young Ralph in a doleful tone as he leaned over his mother's shoulder and looked at the heavily marked verse.

"Ralph," said his mother reproachfully, while the visitor regarded him with a questioning smile, "have you tested it?" she asked. But Ralph, blushing much, had no reply to make.

"Do you know what a hard time the Smiths are having?" said Mrs. Selmser, closing the Bible, as one who had turned to entirely another subject. "Ralph here, found out by accident that they were actually hungry—those children, you know. Doesn't that seem hard? I declare, when I heard how poor little Mamie snatched after a bit of bread, it made the tears come."

Miss Edwards had not heard about them; she asked many questions, and said that directly after Thanksgiving she would go and see them. Then she went away. No sooner was she out of hearing then Mrs. Selmser had something to say. "I was sorry you spoke in that way about the verse, Ralph; if Miss Edwards should ever hear anything about that chicken, she would think you didn't want them to have it."

"She won't ever hear about it," said Ralph; "and besides, you know I said all the time that those chickens were dreadful little to make one do for a big family like ours; Thanksgiving day, too."

"Yes, but, Ralph, you know the Smiths had nothing at all for dinner, and one chicken is better than nothing, isn't it?"

"We might have sent them something else," Ralph said slowly. It had evidently been hard work for him to give up that chicken.

"But we hadn't anything else, my boy, that we could spare, that would have been a kind of a treat to the Smiths. Don't you really think, on the whole, that we did the best we could?"

Ralph gave a little sigh, then looked at his mother and laughed.

"It's all right, Mother," he said, "only you see I had kind of set my heart on our having those two chickens on

Thanksgiving Day all to ourselves; most folks have turkeys, you know, but I told myself I would be contented with chickens, if we could have two of them, and lots of gravy. It isn't for the eating either, that I care so much, it is just because I wanted to be like other folks, you know."

"I understand," the Mother said cheerily, "and you wanted the Smiths to have a good dinner, too; I know just as well as though I could look right into your heart. You wouldn't have had them miss of that chicken for anything, now would you?"

Ralph laughed again, and said he didn't know as he should, and went away whistling. As for Miss Edwards, no sooner was she out of the house, then for some reason she changed her mind, and went at once to call on the Smiths.

Here she heard wonderful stories; they had been in trouble, but they believed their darkest day had passed, thanks to their neighbors. Mrs. Smith constantly wiped away the tears as she told of the many thoughtful kindnesses of Mrs. Selmser and her family. "And they are poor themselves," said Mrs. Smith; "I dare say they had scrimped themselves a good deal to help us all they have."

Miss Edwards did not doubt this, for she knew a good deal about the Selmsers. Their crowning act of kindness, if Miss Smith is to be depended upon, was that chicken. Such a wonderful story as she heard about it! How it, with its companion, had been the special property of Ralph Selmser, the sole survivors of a brood of seven, all the others having come to grief; how Ralph had confided to her boy Peter that he was raising those chickens for their Thanksgiving dinner, and how he and his mother were going to give the Father a surprise; and then to think that they should be willing to change all their plans, and get along with only one chicken for themselves, was almost too much, Mrs. Smith thought. "It isn't as though they had plenty to give," she said, wiping her eyes, "but they have been ready to divide their little with the widow and the fatherless; I hope the Lord will make it up to them."

Mrs. Smith had still more reason for gratitude before that call was concluded, but it is not about her that I want to tell you at present.

I want you to think of Ralph Selmser as looking out of the window on the morning before Thanksgiving, when little Tim Potter, who was everybody's errand boy, appeared in sight, holding on with both hands to the largest turkey Ralph had ever seen. To his great surprise, Tim opened their side gate and squeezed himself and the turkey through it. He rushed to the kitchen door to see what was wanted, and the turkey was laid at his feet in silence, and Tim was off like the wind.

A note was found pinned to the turkey's leg, but when it was examined it said only this: "For Ralph Selmser to give his father and mother a Thanksgiving dinner." And below it, these words: "Trust in the Lord and do good; so shalt thou dwell in the land, and verily thou shalt be fed."

While the others all talked at once, wondering how, and why, Ralph stood back with folded arms, and looked at the turkey.

"It is Grandmother's Bible that did it," he said at last.

# CHAPTER II.

*Take heed, Brethren, lest there be in any of you an*
*evil heart of unbelief, in departing from the*
*living God.*
*Not by might, nor by power, but by my Spirit, saith*
*the Lord of hosts.*
*Great men are not always wise.*
*Thy people shall be my people, and thy God my*
*God.*

The winter set in very gloomily. Ralph, leaning over the kitchen table, listening to his mother while she talked with Mr. Brewster, thought there had never seemed a darker, and could not help thinking privately that his mother was a little, just a little, foolish. Oh! Of course he did not put it in those words, even to himself, but that was what the thought meant, all the same.

This was the way matters stood. Mr. Selmser was out of work, and had been for some time away from home looking for a chance to earn his living; that very morning had come a letter from him saying he had only succeeded in getting enough to do to earn his board, and he saw no prospect in the future, but would hold on a few days longer. Now here sat Mr. Brewster, who had come to offer Ralph's father a place. "I'd be very glad to have him," said the gentleman. "I know him to be a good, steady man, one to be relied upon. It isn't much of a place now, but there might be a better opening before long. We can't tell what may happen."

Mrs. Selmser sewed on, and Ralph wondered what in the world she could mean, and was almost tempted to answer for her. At last she spoke;—

"It isn't the wages, Mr. Brewster, nor the low-down place, as you may say. My husband is not one to wait for good places. He would saw wood for a living, if there wasn't anything else to do, and be thankful to get it. But I don't think he could take this job, even if it came to starving."

Ralph looked amazed, not to say disgusted, and Mr. Brewster, mildly astonished, waited for an explanation.

"You see it is a matter of principle," said Mrs. Selmser. "Reuben doesn't believe in the business, so he oughtn't to help it along."

A patient smile covered Mr. Brewster's face. "Oh, is that the trouble?" he said, in a kindly tone. "Well, my dear madam, you can set your heart at rest; all in the world we shall have for him to do is to cart empty barrels from the manufactory to the warehouse. There certainly cannot be any moral question about that."

Mrs. Selmser's needle flew very fast. "The question is, what goes into the barrels?" she said at last, speaking gently but very firmly.

Mr. Brewster laughed. "I can't imagine what my porter would have to do with such a question," he said, still speaking with a show of kindness. "He is payed for carting barrels, and as I look at it, it is none of his business in any way what is done with them after they leave his hands."

Mrs. Selmser stayed her needle and looked steadily

at her caller.

"It was kind in you to think of us, Mr. Brewster, and I thank you. But I know my husband well enough to be sure that he will have nothing to do with barrels that are going to have beer put into them; so there wouldn't be any use in sending for him."

"Very well, madam," said Mr. Brewster, rising as he spoke. There were two red spots on his cheeks by this time. "I suppose there is no use in my telling you that I think him a very foolish man indeed, and that he will be likely to starve his family before this hard winter is over, if he tries to live by such a squeamish conscience as that. But my duty is done, so I will bid you good evening."

"Mother," said Ralph, almost before the door closed after him, "I don't see how you dared to say that to Mr. Brewster. He is a very great man—the greatest man in this town. The boys said today that he was the richest man in the country."

"I have nothing to do with that," said Mrs. Selmser. "I had to answer him, and there was nothing to say, as I look at things."

"But don't you think you are a little bit—a little bit" said Ralph, hesitating for a word, and leaving a blank at last. "You know Father wouldn't have to touch beer, and as Mr. Brewster said, what is it to him what goes into the barrels?"

"What difference does it make with you, my son, if a boy in school borrows your knife to cut a hole in his desk, and you know what he is going to do, yet you open your knife and hand it to him?"

"That's different," said Ralph.

"Yes, it is," said his mother, "because the mischief would only be done to a piece of wood, while beer now,—" and she, too, left her sentence blank.

"Come," she said, after a few minutes of silence, "read the verses and we will have prayers, without waiting for Mary Jane. She said she would be late tonight. They are getting ready for a Christmas dinner, you know."

"It is more than we are doing," said Ralph, with a sigh. "I don't see how we are to have any kind of dinners if Father can't get work. Shall I read some marked verses, Mother?"

"Yes, do," said Mrs. Selmser. "Let us have some of Mother's good words tonight to help us, and don't you worry about the dinners, Ralph. Don't you remember one of the verses—'Verily, thou shalt be fed'?"

"One would think Mr. Brewster ought to know right from wrong," said Ralph, with another sigh. "He is a great man."

Then he turned, without much thought about it, to the very first marked verse on which his eyes alighted, "Great men are not always wise."

"Why," said Ralph in astonishment, "isn't that strange? Did you know that was in the Bible, Mother? Why do you suppose Grandmother marked that?"

"Maybe she had something to do with great men herself, some time," said Mrs. Selmser, with a pleasant smile. She was very glad that Ralph had found that verse. A lesson that he needed very much to learn was that it took more than money to make greatness.

A few minutes more and the short earnest prayer had

been offered, the door locked, the fire covered for the night, and the kitchen deserted. Meantime, Mary Jane had sent word by a neighbor, that there were so many "last" things to do, in order to be ready for the next day, she had decided to stay all night and help them through.

Ralph could not help another sigh as he turned to give a last look at the room. It was in perfect order, not looking at all, the boy thought, as a room should look on Christmas Eve. One solitary stocking hung by the chimney corner. All the little Selmsers had agreed that Baby, as the three-year-old Ned was called, was the only one who could afford to hang up his stocking this year. "Ned is too young to understand things," the Mother said, "but the rest of you do, and will be cheerful and good, I know. Next year maybe we can have the chimney corner full of stockings." So Ned's hung alone. It had been a perplexing thing to fill that stocking, and had really taken hours of contriving. Every member of the family had some odd thing to put in it. When they were all stuffed in, and it was found to be quite filled, I think everyone felt a sense of relief. But the stocking did look lonely to Ralph as he gave it a last look; and though he said not a word, he thought in his heart that he would like very well to hang his beside it, for company. He told himself, as he climbed upstairs, that he didn't see any sign of ever being able to hang up his stocking again, or to have any nice Christmases. They were growing poorer and poorer; if Father did not get work soon, he did not see what would become of them.

And so night settled down on the little home, and the embers of the dying fire lighted the room. But the stocking by the chimney corner was not so lonely, after they were all gone, as Ralph imagined. Certain strange little visitors came out of their houses and eyed it curiously, and sighed because it was beyond their reach. They would have liked so much to gnaw it! And they too grumbled over this Christmas Eve, and said, "They might as well live in a barn; there was nothing to be had in this house worth nibbling for!" But they had no marked verses on which to stay their courage.

The sunshine of the next morning had not yet conquered the frost on the window-pane, when Ralph, who was making a fire for his mother, heard a brisk voice call his name. "Ralph, my boy, has your Father come home?"

"No, sir," said Ralph, dropping his armful of wood, and turning to open the door for Mr. Powell, who was coming up the walk. "He is in Barton."

"Has he found work yet?"

"No, sir. Mother had a letter last night, saying he did not know of anything yet."

"Glad of it," said Mr. Powell, and as this did not sound like a very friendly thing to say, Ralph did not know how to answer it, so was quiet, and by this time Mrs. Selmser had heard the voices and come to the door.

"Good morning!" said Mr. Powell, talking fast. "Can you give me just the address to reach your husband quickly, by telegram? Ralph tells me he has not found employment, and I want to get hold of him as quickly as possible. My foreman has given me the slip, without a day's warning. I suppose he thinks I cannot fill his place, and so will have to bid higher, but I have been wishing for a good chance to get your husband in the place. I have had my eye on him for a year, but didn't see any chance of an opening, so long as the other behaved himself, but now that he hasn't, it is all right. I will telegraph your husband to come home by the noon train, so you better have a Christmas dinner all ready for him. Just send around to our supply store, madam, for anything you want. I guess you will find everything there, and your husband will probably deal with me, after this. I supply all my people at cost. Brewster told me last night you had refused a place for your husband in his brewery. Glad of it. That's the grit I like. He won't lose anything, I guess. I pay my foreman a good salary, and it is a permanent place if a true man wants it."

Mr. Powell talked fast, and made a short stay. He was the largest business man in town, and was always in a hurry, but it seemed to Ralph he would never go. The boy wanted to throw up his hat to the ceiling and shout, and stand on one foot and whirl on the other, and dance what he called a "jig", and none of these things seemed exactly proper to do in Mr. Powell's presence.

"Oh Mother, Mother!" he said, as soon as he could get breath again, after all these things were finally accomplished, "some great men are wise, anyhow, and Mr. Powell is a great deal greater than Mr. Brewster ever thought of being. Why, Mother, he pays his foreman as much as a thousand dollars a year! Oh, Mother! What if you had told Mr. Brewster Father would come and move his old beer bottles! Wouldn't that have been just awful?"

# CHAPTER III.

*The voice of one crying in the wilderness, prepare*
*ye the way of the Lord.*
*As His custom was, He went into the synagogue on*
*the Sabbath day.*
*As soon as He had spoken, immediately the leprosy*
*departed from him and he was cleansed.*
*Who forgiveth all thine iniquities, who healeth all*
*thy diseases.*

Ralph moved restlessly about the room, not seeming able to settle anything. The little girls were ready for church, and his mother had twice told him that he would be late, before he made up his mind to speak: "I don't believe I'll go to church today, Mother."

"Are you sick?" his mother asked, pausing in the midst of her bustling about, and looking at him anxiously.

"No, ma'am, not sick exactly, but you know I have a cold," he said, giving a little cough, as if to prove his words. "I don't feel just like going, somehow."

"Well," said Mrs. Selmser, speaking with a little hesitation, as one who didn't half-like what she was going to say, "you know we like to have all the family about us in church, and it ought to be an important reason that keeps one at home, but then, if you don't feel well enough to go, that is reason enough. You are sure you have not a sore throat?" and she looked at him anxiously.

"Oh, no, ma'am! My throat isn't sore a bit; it is just a cold, you know." And again he tried that little cough.

"Well," said Mrs. Selmser again, "I suppose you will have to stay at home. But what will you do all the morning? Perhaps I would better stay with you."

"Oh, no, indeed," Ralph said, "I wouldn't have you do that for anything. I can get along all right. I've got a nice book to read."

Mrs. Selmser did not look as pleased as she might have done over this bit of news. "The Bible is the best book to read on Sunday when people cannot go to church," she said gravely.

"Oh! I shall read the Bible," Ralph answered eagerly. "I'm going to read my chapter the first thing, and some of my marked verses, before I open my Sunday-school book."

"And live up to them? Reading Bible verses doesn't amount to much you know, unless you do what they say."

"Why, of course," said Ralph, but he spoke less confidently than before. He knew enough about the Bible to realize that it was sometimes a hard book to live up to.

In another hour the family were all gone, and Ralph was alone in the neat kitchen, with the fire burning brightly, and his attractive-looking book on his lap. He had read a few pages in it the night before, but he did not himself realize how much this had had to do with his not feeling well enough to go to church. His friend Bennie Stone, had given it to him on Saturday morning, to return to the library for him, and secure another, because he was going to his grandmother's to spend Sunday, and could not do it for himself. Ralph had not looked into the book until night, and then, as I say, had found it delightful. All the while he was undressing, he tried to plan how he might read that book. He could not draw it from the school, because it would be his turn tomorrow to have a book for which he had been waiting several weeks. If he let this opportunity pass, there was no telling when he would have another. It was just as he was hopping into bed, that the thought came to him: "If I shouldn't happen to be well enough to go to church tomorrow morning, I might read it then."

On the whole, I do not think it strange that by morning he thought himself not very well. The book lay on his lap, but Ralph was mindful of his promise, and reached for Grandmother's Bible. First his chapter—he was reading the Bible through in course. The chapter for the day proved to be almost entirely composed of proper names. Ralph tried to give them attention, but could not help thinking how uninteresting they were. Now, for the marked verse; he decided that he would read only one today, and that he would take it from the Gospels—the first marked verse he saw. This was the verse: "As the custom was, he went into the synagogue on the Sabbath day." Ralph read it through twice before he began to realize what "living up" to this verse was going to mean to him.

Gradually the thought shaped itself in his mind: "That verse is about Jesus, and to live up to it, I must do as near like it as I can. Well, don't I, I should like to know? When have I stayed away from church before? A fellow can't go to church when he has a cold. Disturb all the people coughing. Poh! Ralph Selmser, what's the use? You know you haven't coughed but three times this morning; and two of those you could of smothered if you wanted to. And you know if it was Monday, and there was a coasting spree on the hill, you would coax like a good fellow, to go, and know forty reasons why it wouldn't hurt you." Were there two people talking? Ralph felt a little curious about it himself; they seemed to hold such different views; but he knew this much: both of them lived in his heart. Silence for a few minutes, during which time Ralph read the marked verse again. Then he rose up, stretched himself, looked in the glass in the clock face to make sure that his hair was all right, and made this remark: "It is my opinion, Ralph Selmser, that you had better do 'as your custom is', and make for church as fast as your legs can carry you."

It was during the singing of the second hymn that he slipped past his father and took a seat at his mother's side. For the benefit of those interested, I want to report that he did not cough once during the service.

"What has become of your cold?" asked his mother after the benediction was pronounced.

"Gone," he answered with a odd smile.

"There was a verse in Grandmother's Bible that cured it."

Mrs. Selmser asked no more questions; in some respect she was a wise woman. On the way home from church she said she shouldn't wonder if Mother's Bible would be worth a fortune to the children.

# CHAPTER IV.

*If any man hath ears to hear, let him hear.*
*Go home to thy friends, and tell them how great*
*things the Lord hath done for thee, and hath had*
*compassion on thee.*
*Be not afraid, only believe.*
*And they went out and preached that men should*
*repent.*

"Ho!" said Ralph, pausing over a verse that was heavily marked with blue ink, "this is a little bit of a fellow, and it doesn't seem to say anything. Grandma marked it, though, as if she thought it was made of gold."

"What is the verse?" Mrs. Selmser asked, with a somewhat unsteady voice; there came to her just then a memory of her dear old mother bending over the golden verses, getting wealth from them; and it made her heart ache so for a sight of the Mother's face, that it seemed for a few minutes as though she could not wait any longer.

"It is 'Be-not-afraid-only-believe,' " said Ralph, running the words together as though they were one, and making only a comma at the close.

"Why, that is a lovely verse, I am sure."

"Well, it doesn't say anything; doesn't finish, you know. What is a fellow to believe?"

"A boy who belongs to the Lord can use the verse in a great many ways. I heard a minister say once it was a blank check, ready to use for any sum that was needed. Believe that God can take care of you anywhere, no matter what happens. Don't you see?"

"Y—e—s'—m," Ralph said, with a slow drawl, "but then I don't understand such a wholesale verse very well; it's short, though, and I'm going to take it for mine."

All day long he didn't give the verse a thought. He was busy in school, and at home, and was bright and happy; whistling most of the time when alone, and forgetting that there was such a thing as trouble in the world, or that he had occasion for anybody's help. However, he succeeded in offending three boys younger than himself who were generally in mischief of some sort. They planned a bit of mischief for this particular day, which Ralph discovered in time, and spoiled. They were very angry about it, and promised to "be even with him." Ralph laughed, and whistled, and wondered what the chaps thought they could do.

By dark he found out.

It was Ralph's duty to close the windows of the schoolrooms, after they had been swept and dusted, see that all was in order for the night, and close the heavy doors that locked with spring locks. He was whistling through the hall, attending to his work, just as twilight was falling; the sweeper had been delayed, and it was later than usual. Three empty coal hoods stood by the door of the coal cellar. Ralph swung them all over his arm, it being his duty to leave them in the cellar. First he took the precaution to fasten back the heavy outside door lest a gust of wind might blow it shut. It fastened with a chain and hasp, so no wind could possibly loosen it; then he went swiftly down the steep stairs, whistling, "See the conquering hero comes."

"No, he doesn't!" murmured a low voice outside. "He goes, but he doesn't 'come' so quickly as he thinks. Now, Jim, is your time; swing to the door; there's nobody in sight." And Jim pushed, keeping Rob back with one hand, lest he should rattle the chain and give Ralph warning in time to escape.

The door closed with a dull thud that stopped the whistling below. Ralph was just ready to spring up the steps into daylight again. The minute he heard that thud, he knew that he was a prisoner; though how the door had gotten loose he could not imagine. It wasn't a pleasant prospect for a boy, this being shut into a great dark cellar, with stone walls and rats for company; feeling pretty certain that the long night would have to wear away, and perhaps a great part of the next day before he would be discovered.

In fact it might be several days; for he remembered with sudden terror that it was Friday night, and the cellar need not be entered again, probably would not be until Monday. What should he do? Which way turn? Would it be possible for him to live in that damp, dark spot until he was found? Could he hope to make noise enough to attract the attention of any passer-by? But that was folly; the building stood back from the road, in the center of large grounds, and the cellar was at the back part of the building. It was then and there, sitting on the lowest step of the cellar stairs, with his elbows on his knees, and his head in his hands, that Ralph thought again of the marked

verse: "Be not afraid, only believe." He was afraid; then he owned it to himself. Were the words for him?

If he only knew what to believe! He wished he had talked longer with his mother about it. He did believe in the great God, and wanted to be His servant. But was he expected to believe that God would plan some way to get him out of that cellar that night? "How could He!" said poor Ralph to himself. "Nobody comes to the building nights, let alone the cellars. I've just got to stay here, of course; but, oh, dear, it is dreadful! What will Mother think? They will all be scared; and they won't know where to look for me, because I ran home, between times, while I was waiting for the dusting, and I didn't tell them I'd got to go back to the schoolhouse. They will think I'm in the river, and they'll go to dragging it and have an awful time; and here I am in this dreadful cellar! Oh, dear! I wish I knew what to believe."

His mother's voice seemed to sound in his ears: "Believe that God will take care of you anywhere, no matter what happens." Those were the very words she said. Did he believe it? If he did, why was he afraid? A few minutes passed, which seemed like hours to Ralph, then he got down on the coal grimed floor and prayed this prayer:—

"Dear Lord, I'm in awful trouble; I never was before, but this is awful! I can't help being some afraid. But I believe in Thy power to keep me safe, even here. Oh, Lord! Take care of me, and comfort Mother, for Jesus' sake. Amen!"

You will notice that his faith was not strong enough to pray to be let out of the cellar. He believed that to be such an exceedingly improbable thing as to be almost impossible.

Yet, as the long slow minutes dragged along, he heard a sound, and started up and listened as for his life. Was it rats? No, it came from overhead. Was it burglars? Then would they come to the cellar and finding him kill him? The cold sweat stood in great drops on the poor boy's face. The heavy door was certainly being tampered with; he heard the grating of a key in the lock; he heard it slowly swing back on its hinges; he saw the glimmer of a lantern. Should he try to hide? No, he wouldn't; instead he almost laughed aloud in his sudden relief. The tall form of Professor Fordham was coming down the stairs.

"It's only me, Professor," he shouted, as the startled gentleman paused half-way down; "It's only me, Ralph Selmser. I got shut in; but how came you to come and let me out?"

"What does all this mean?" said the Professor, setting down his lantern. Then there were explanations to make. When Ralph had told as much as he knew of his own story, Professor Fordham said he had been called to the coal cellar to look at a flue that the janitor thought needed attention; that he had stooped down on his hands and knees to examine it, and that when he reached home he missed a pocketbook that was filled with important papers; not finding it anywhere else, he had thought of the coal cellar, and came at once to look for it.

And Ralph, as he hunted about by the light of the lantern, and finally picked up the lost book, said in an awe-stricken tone: "How easy He did it! And I thought

He couldn't!"

"Did what, my boy?" asked the professor. Then Ralph's pale face flushed a little, as he said, "I was just thinking out loud, Professor. You see I thought the Lord would take care of me here, all night, but I didn't believe He could plan any way to let me out, before morning, anyhow, and He did it just as easy! Mother will think that it all came about through Grandmother's verses; and maybe it did. I'm afraid Mother is awfully scared. What time is it, Professor Fordham?"

"A little after six," said the Professor, and Ralph in great astonishment owned that he thought it was about midnight.

Then they walked home; but I believe you will be glad to hear that Professor Fordham said, when he left Ralph, "We must look into this matter. Doors that are chained back don't close without hands. I saw three boys skulking about where they ought not to be, and have my suspicions; tomorrow we will see what we can discover."

# CHAPTER V.

*Whosoever will come after me, let him deny himself,*
*and take up his cross and follow me.*
*Whosoever shall not receive the Kingdom of God as*
*a little child, he shall not enter therein.*
*Suffer little children to come unto me, and forbid*
*them not, for of such is the kingdom of God.*
*Thou Son of David, have mercy on me.*

Ralph rocked back and forth in the little wooden rocker in front of the fireplace, and turned the leaves of the big Bible in search of his verse for the next day.

"Here is one that I like," he said at last, "because it is marked with red ink. I like red ink best, and I'd just as soon choose it; that is, it would be easy enough one, only it isn't likely I could use it; it doesn't fit me."

"How can you tell what verse will fit you tomorrow?" asked his mother. "Read it to me."

So Ralph read: "Whosoever will come after me, let him deny himself, and take up his cross and follow me."

"And you think that doesn't fit you? Why not? You don't mean, I hope, that you don't belong to those who want to follow Him?"

"Oh, no!" said Ralph promptly; "I don't mean that, of course. But, you see, I haven't got anything to deny myself. I go to school now, and I like to go; and my lessons are nice, and I like to study them; and I don't have anything to do that I wouldn't just as like to do as not. A few months ago it might have fitted me; I had to keep denying myself lots of things I wanted to do, but now it's different."

Mrs. Selmser smiled a peculiar smile, and sewed away for some minutes before she spoke again.

"If I were you I would take it, Ralph. I never heard of anybody who really wanted to live by it that didn't have chances enough. You can't tell, you see, what tomorrow may do."

Ralph laughed lightly. "I ain't afraid," he said. "Tomorrow's Saturday, and I'm going to give Ned a ride on my sled, and I'm going to get green things and berries for Mary Jane to trim up the room for Father's birthday; and there isn't a thing to do all day but I'd rather do than not. But then, I'll take it and see."

"Fire! Fire! Fire!" It was that sound repeated by shrill voices that awoke Ralph several hours later.

"Tomorrow" had already begun; it was almost two o'clock. Out tumbled Ralph in eager haste, and was ready, by the time his father was, to start in search of the fire. It was a stormy night; a wild March wind was blowing, and the air was full of fast whirling snow. Great crowds had gathered at the scene of the fire, and a wild and beautiful scene it was. Ralph stood and watched the flames, filled with a feeling that, to say the least, was not regret, when he discovered that the house, which was evidently going to burn to the ground, was the home where his tormenters lived! The very boys who had shut him into the school cellar, and were always doing something to annoy him.

"It isn't any fault of mine," he said sturdily,

ashamed that there was a little feeling of gladness in his heart, and yet trying to apologize for it. "I wouldn't have set their house on fire for anything in this world; and I'd put it out, quicker, if I could. But since its got to burn, I'm glad it belongs to such mean chaps as they, instead of to the fellows I like."

"Get out!" said a man just at Ralph's elbow. He had been working with a will, and had just stopped for breath. He explained the meaning of his words to a man who was with him.

"It's that little cat; she's under my feet most of the time. Look at her! She's scared to death, and the smoke makes her blind. She'll get killed here if nobody looks after her. Look at those sparks! They are going to catch on the side roof now!" And the men were off.

Ralph stood still and looked, not at the flames, but at the "little cat". The special pet of those two boys! Once he told his mother that he believed "those fellows liked their ridiculous kitten better than they did their little baby sister." Now she was dashing about in a wild way, right under the feet of the flying firemen, and was certainly in a fair way to be killed.

"Serve 'em right, too," declared Ralph. "Think how they treated my Towser only the other night; humph! Think how they treated me." Again there came into his heart that glad feeling. He wouldn't have hurt the "little cat" for anything; but he knew he was glad she was likely to be hurt. Suddenly there came to him a thought so surprising that he whistled, even there, with the flames rising higher every minute. Wasn't it his duty to "deny himself" that glad feeling and "take up his cross" and that little cat and carry her home out of harm's way?

"Pshaw!" he said aloud. "Likely story that a Bible verse would have anything to do with a cat! What kind of denying would that be, anyhow? As if I wanted their old kitten to be killed, if she can keep herself from it."

No use, Ralph. Bible verses apply to smaller creatures than cats; and you know as well as you need to know, that a follower of Him whose words you are quoting, would be merciful to the smallest and weakest of His creatures.

Suddenly Ralph gave a dart into the midst of the smoke, being pushed aside and scolded by an impatient fireman, and being promptly ordered home by his own father, who had dashed into the worst of it, and was helping fight the fire. Ralph went home, very sorry to miss the rest of the fire; but the "little cat" trembling as though she had a chill, was tucked close to his breast, wrapped under his stout overcoat. He had denied himself the feeling of satisfaction over the thought that something belonging to those scamp of boys had come to grief.

Perhaps you think the boys were very grateful the next day when they found their pet had been saved. This was the way they told the story:

"And don't you think, with all the rest, we came pretty near losing Spot. That Ralph Selmser came prowling around and walked off with her under his coat, as large as you please! No telling what he would have done with her, only one of the men saw him and told Father, and he went himself and brought her home. As if it wasn't enough to have our house burn down, but we must have things stolen! Ralph pretends that he took her to save her, because she was dashing right into the fire, and he heard a man say she would have been killed; but that is stuff and nonsense; as if a cat didn't know how to take care of herself."

So that was their gratitude!

But when Ralph heard of it, he laughed, and said to his mother: "I'll have to hold on to the verse, Mother. I'm going to deny myself the pleasure of knocking both those fellows over, and it feels kind of pleasant to hold myself in; I rather like it. But you see if I had let that little cat kill herself, I should have felt just awful. It's strange that Bible verses belong even to cats!"

# CHAPTER VI.

*Rejoice greatly, O daughter of Zion; O daughter of
   Jerusalem; behold, thy King cometh unto thee.*
*He came unto his own, and his own received him
   not.*
*Love is the fulfilling of the law.*
*But I say unto you, that in this place is One greater
   than the Temple.*

"Ho!" said Ralph, "I've got a speck of a verse this
time, and I don't see much sense to it, I must say."

"Read it out," said his mother, sewing rapidly. "It
must be a strange verse if it hasn't much sense. Is it one
of Grandmother's?"

"Oh, yes! Marked round and round. One, two,
three—it is just seven words: 'Love is the fulfilling of the
law.' "

"It has plenty of sense, I think. What does it say to
you?"

"Why, it says," said Ralph, laughing, "that if I love
you, it doesn't make any matter whether I mind you or
not. Well, if that's true, it's a nice idea. Shall we try it,
Mother? I'll agree to love you, right straight through,
and then you won't care about the minding, you see."

"But I don't see any such thing. It doesn't say that
to me, Ralph; and no more it didn't to Grandmother; she
was very particular about the minding. What it says is,
that if you love folks enough, you will be sure to keep

their laws, just because you love them."

"S'pose their laws aren't worth keeping?"

"Yes, I see," said Mrs. Selmser, stopping to bite the end of her thread, "my explanation wasn't good; there's no 'supposing' any such thing in this case, because it's talking about His laws, and all of them are worth keeping."

"Well," said Ralph, after a thoughtful pause, "I don't see how that would make a boy keep to rules, and things."

"Just you try it tomorrow," his mother said, "and see how many things that verse will fit."

"Tomorrow" was one of the worst days in the year for a boy to keep in exactly the right track. It was "April fool's day", and it seemed to be well named; for every boy at least, as well as some girls, acted as foolish as possible.

Being a boy, and as full of fun as any of them, Ralph had his temptations, but, on the whole, got through the day pretty well, and congratulated himself on the way home, that he had had "lots of fun, and hadn't done anything very dreadful, either."

Just around the corner, on Newton Street, he came plump upon Jerry Smith.

Jerry had set up business but a short time before, and was doing his best to make a living, selling bunches of early spring flowers, choice bits of moss, and lichen, and indeed anything he could find in the woods or out of it, to sell. He really worked very hard; sometimes under most discouraging circumstances; having been known to tramp all day long without making a penny. On this particular occasion he looked very funny indeed to Ralph. He was barefooted, though the spring day was not any too warm for comfort; he had seated himself in the shelter of a wall, his hat had fallen off, his mouth had fallen open, and Jerry was fast asleep. Poor fellow, he had been up since daylight working hard, and selling little; this was one of his bad days.

But the only thought Ralph had at first, was how funny the fellow looked sitting there in broad daylight, sound asleep. After a moment, came another thought. Jerry's mouth stood so invitingly open. What if he should pop into it the brown bug he was carrying home for Miss Edward's collection! He could easily get her another, and what delicious fun it would be to see Jerry jump and sputter, and sneeze, and all but choke over that unexpected morsel.

"It's a clean little fellow, and not poison, nor anything."

This Ralph explained to himself, in reply to seven inconvenient words which came suddenly to mind—Grandmother's marked words: "Love is the fulfilling of the law."

"Pshaw!" he added impatiently as the seven words kept repeating themselves in a kind of steady undertone. "What sense is there in saying that, all the while. As if this bug had anything to do with 'love' or law, and as if the law was about Jerry, anyhow. I know all the Commandments, and there isn't a word in them about a bug. It isn't a bad bug, and he won't swallow it, either, of course."

It's of no use, Ralph. You know too much about

"Grandmother's Bible" to be caught by any such weak arguments. As distinctly as though that had been his verse for the day instead of the other, there came trooping into Ralph's mind the words: "Whatsoever ye would that men should do to you, do ye even so to them."

Here was a law not in the Ten Commandments in so many words, but spoken by the same voice of authority.

"Well," said Ralph reflectively, "I'm not afraid of brown bugs—not nice clean fellows like this one. I wouldn't mind, maybe." The last word put in as a sort of afterthought, spoken more slowly than the others. He worked the toe of his strong old shoe deep into the mud while he stood and thought. Visions of himself in Jerry's place, came to him; Jerry who had probably had very little breakfast, and no dinner to speak of; Jerry, barefooted, and shivery, trying to sell things that people didn't want; Jerry who had no nice hot supper waiting for him at home. If such a strange thing should happen as that he should ever sit on a street corner asleep under like circumstances, would he like to have a fat brown bug put slyly into his open mouth by a giggling boy? That was the question.

"No," said this honest boy slowly, "I just wouldn't."

Well, then, "Love is the fulfilling of the law." Did he love Jerry enough to obey this law for his sake, and forego his fun? The fact was, he didn't believe that he loved Jerry at all; Jerry might be well enough for those who liked him, but Ralph had never exactly approved of him in any way.

Suddenly a curious look came into the boy's eyes.

Just at that moment this question dawned upon him: Ralph Selsmer, do you love the Lord Jesus Christ enough to fulfill His law? It is that wonderful Jesus who cares about Jerry Smith, and would not have an uncomfortable thing done to him. If you do honestly love Him, you will fulfill His law even in what you consider so small a matter as this.

Back went the bug into Ralph's pocket. It had had a narrow escape, but Miss Edwards was sure of it now for her collection. Ralph dived his hand into the other pocket and drew therefrom a lovely square of golden gingerbread. He had been pumping water for Mrs. Ebenezer Tucker, and she had given him a large piece of gingerbread in return. Carefully he broke off a generous "chunk" and deftly poked it into Jerry's open mouth, then dodged behind a corner.

"Ah! Ugh! Whissch!" sputtered Jerry, sitting up straight and bringing both hands to his mouth to remove the obstruction. Then he stared at it, then rubbed his eyes and looked about him in all directions, a much bewildered boy. Suddenly a broad smile spread over his freckled face.

"I'm blessed," he said aloud, "if I haven't been asleep, and there's been an April shower, and it has rained gingerbread!"

Whereupon he put the chunk back into his large mouth.

# CHAPTER VII.

*Take ye heed, watch and pray; for you know not*
*when the time is.*
*She hath done what she could.*
*This do in remembrance of Me.*
*Betrayest thou the Son of man with a kiss?*

Ralph was in a very happy state of mind.

He had just reached home from an evening spent at the Barwood's elegant home; the handsomest place in town. He had had an elegant supper and been shown all sorts of kind attention from the young ladies of the house, and altogether he felt quite satisfied with himself, and eager to tell his mother and Mary Jane the whole story.

"It's the biggest hall I ever saw," he explained. "It isn't just a hall, you know; they have seats in it, great big old fashioned arm chairs, and there are pictures and bronze statues and all sorts of things.

"There is one strange looking fellow in bronze, standing by the hall window, that is just as natural as life. I declare, I couldn't help thinking some of the time that he was alive. But he had a horrid face. I don't know why anybody should want an image of him, I'm sure.

"Mary Jane, it is well you were not there; you would have been scared dreadfully over the dog; he's the biggest dog I ever saw. His name is Nero. He goes out with Miss Elice when she takes a walk. Miss Elice is

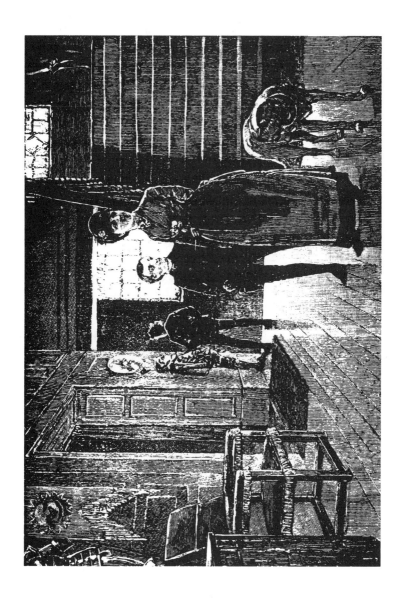

Sherman's sister, you know; she seems more like his mother. I guess he has to ask her about things just as though she were; his mother is dead, you see. But I do wish you could see that splendid hall and those lovely wide stairs, and the curtain at the top and everything."

Ralph drew a sigh of satisfaction, and stopped for breath. Then Mary Jane asked a question.

"How came Sherman Barwood to ask you home with him, all of a sudden?"

"How should I know?" answered Ralph, a little uneasily. "Because he wanted to, I suppose. He's lonesome in that great big house, I guess. Some of the boys go home with him quite often."

"But he never asked you before," continued his sister, "and he is older than you, isn't he?"

"Not so very much," said Ralph, turning the leaves of the big Bible. "Mother, where shall I read tonight?" Then as though Mary Jane's question annoyed him a little, he returned to them with a half laugh: "Of course, Mary Jane, if he were ever going to invite me, there would have to be a first time."

"Is he a good boy, Ralph?" asked Mrs. Selmser, looking up from her busy needle at the boy's flushed face for a moment.

"Good enough, I guess," spoken rather reluctantly. Then, catching his mother's eye, "Well I mean—sometimes I think he is not so very honest about things. Gets a peek into his books if he can, you know, and wants lots of the fellows to do that. Here's a verse marked in green ink; how strange it looks! stand well in class without digging for it. But Grandmother hardly ever used green ink. 'Take ye heed, watch and pray; for you know not when the time is.' That time hasn't come yet, has it? What an awful while those men would have had to wait if they had lived till now. I'm glad they found out about it without waiting so long."

Mary Jane laughed; her brother's ideas often seemed to her very strange; but Mrs. Selmser was still looking sober over what Ralph had said before.

"I don't suppose they had to wait long for a chance to use the first part of the verse," she said significantly, "and for that matter, the last half could be used to fit into everyday life. We don't know when the Lord is coming, that's something to watch for; but we don't know when danger is coming to us and we need to watch and pray about that. Maybe you need to do it over Sherman Barwood and his sudden friendship for you. I don't think I care to have you very great friends with a boy who isn't strictly honest and honorable if he does live in such a grand house."

"Oh, Mother!" said Ralph. But having made this answer he found he had nothing more to say just then. He chose the first verse of the reading for his because his mother wanted him to do so, not because he felt that he needed to watch especially, and went off to bed presently quite satisfied with himself and his friendship with Sherman Barwood.

Neither did he take any special heed in that direction. On the contrary he met the handsome boy's kindness more than half-way and winked at or endured in silence several things which he knew were wrong, calling them to himself "not exactly right", instead of that short plain word "wrong."

There came a day when he had reason to remember his verse, and his mother's warning, and Mary Jane's questions.

There was no getting away from the fact that he was in serious trouble. The spring examinations were drawing near; every boy in his class was very anxious indeed to get into the next grade and some of them were very much afraid they would not.

"If a fellow could get a peep at the examination questions that are lying all this while in Professor Morehead's desk he might know which way to turn to get ready," said Sherman Barwood one evening, when Ralph had gone home with him to get a certain book he had been promised, and was lingering to enjoy the beauty and the luxury about him. He often went home with Sherman Barwood nowadays; was indeed quite as intimate with him as any boy in the school, and could not help being just a little proud of Sherman's evident fondness for his society.

"Are they there?" asked Ralph, in a interested tone.

"Oh yes! Safe and sound. Tucked away in that black covered book which shuts with a rubber band. I saw the Professor look them over the other day, then rubber them up in that book and push them in under the papers on the right hand, as though he was afraid if he didn't bury them deep enough some of us fellows would peep through the key hole and get an idea."

Ralph laughed.

"I wish we could," he said carelessly. "Especially I'd like a peep at the philosophy questions; just enough to know which section the most of them were from. I feel the shakiest in that direction of any."

"I don't see what particular harm it would do to let us know what section we are to be examined in," said Sherman, still with an air of one who was only interested because his friend was. "They don't expect the class to be equally well posted on the entire book, of course; if they would just hint which sections to review most carefully it might help us and be all right enough, for what I can see."

Ralph laughed. He could 'see' that it wouldn't be right at all, but what was the use in saying so? Of course Sherman didn't mean that, anyway.

Well, the days passed, and one evening Ralph was called to Professor Morehead's room and asked some questions and told some facts which perfectly overwhelmed him.

It was quite a long interview, but I can give it to you in a few words. The examination papers had been tampered with, some of them; among the others the philosophy questions had been, the professor had reason to think, copied. Certain scraps of paper had been found which made him pretty sure of it and which also led him to fear he knew something about who had done it.

Then he asked the astonished Ralph a few bewildering questions:

"Are you a particular friend of Sherman Barwood?"

"Why," said Ralph, blushing, he could hardly have told for what reason, "I am pretty well acquainted with him."

"And you go to his house quite often? Were you

there on Tuesday evening last?" Ralph considered and
said that he was. "Did you and Sherman have some talk
about the examination papers?"

"Yes, sir." Ralph knew now that his face was very
red indeed.

"And did you say that you would like to see the
philosophy papers; that you felt shaky about that study;
and that you thought it would be fair enough to get an
idea of what section they were drawn from chiefly?"

"No, sir," said Ralph eagerly. "I did not say that;
not that last part. I—you see, sir, he—well, we both had
been talking about the examination, and—"

And Ralph went through the story as well as he
could, floundering a good deal, embarrassed by his very
effort to recall his exact words, and to make the matter
entirely plain to Professor Morehead; confused, also, by
the feeling that he was not succeeding. He had been
interrupted at last. The Professor had assured him that
that was all he wished to know; that he had more clues
now than he needed; that it was his duty to tell Ralph that
some very grave testimony had been brought against
himself, but that he might rest assured the matter should
be shifted to the utmost and the truth discovered if
possible.

Then Ralph had gone home to his mother with a
choking feeling at his throat and indignation too great for
tears. Do you wonder that as he turned the leaves of
Grandmother's Bible he stooped over the marked verse
"Betrayest thou the Son of man with a kiss?" And felt
that he could understand something of the bitterness of
that awful betrayal by his own experience? Had not

Sherman Barwood done something a little like it to him? Getting his confidence and then repeating the words that he had said carelessly as though they were in earnest, and even adding to them words of his own which Ralph had not thought of saying.

Oh! If he had only "taken heed" as his mother and Mary Jane hinted might be necessary, and not been so vain over this friendship, he might never had fallen into this terrible trouble and disgrace.

As it was, it seemed to the poor fellow that he could not possibly wait for the investigation which Professor Morehead had promised.

# CHAPTER VIII.

*They hated me without a cause.*
*Pilate saith unto them, take ye him and crucify*
*him.*
*He humbled himself, and became obedient unto*
*death, even the death of the cross.*
*Now is Christ risen from the dead, and become the*
*first-fruits of them that slept.*

Ralph Selmser never forgot the days which immediately followed the discovery that he was suspected of stealing examination papers. He put the charge to himself in that bald way to try to get used to the misery of it. He, Ralph Selmser, whose word had always been taken, at home, without the slightest hesitation! It was almost impossible to realize that anybody could believe him guilty of so mean a thing.

Yet some people evidently did. More and more, as the days passed, and the story leaked out in some mysterious way, as stories will, the boys drew off from him, until sometimes it seemed to the poor fellow that he had not a friend. He had gone in haste and indignation to Sherman Barwood; but when that young fellow was indignantly asked what he meant by repeating the nonsense they had talked together as though it had been earnest, even forgetting which of them said certain things, he shrugged his handsome shoulders and said he did not see how he was expected to know when a fellow was in fun and when he was in earnest; that certainly he was the only one who had been heard to say he wanted to get hold of the philosophy examination papers; and now that they had been gotten hold of by somebody, what was one to think?

Ralph was so utterly dumfounded over the discovery that his supposed friend actually believed him to have been guilty of such a thing, that he turned away without another word.

In this way the friendship was broken; and poor Ralph moped at home when the other boys were at play; and grew so pale and troubled looking that his mother wished the matter could be settled without further waiting; and wished every day that "Father," who had gone on a long business journey for Mr. Powell, was only at home to advise their boy what to do. Meantime, by dint of earnest questioning and much watching, Ralph had discovered that the boys who had fastened him into the cellar were witnesses against him.

Something they had seen, or heard, or imagined, made out a grave charge, over which the faculty were puzzling, trying to get at the truth. In the meantime Dr. Welborne, the chief of the faculty, was absent, and nothing definite could be done until his return.

"What does make those boys so determined to injure you?" Mary Jane asked one evening, as for the hundredth time the whole story had been gone over, and Ralph had pieced together bits of all he had heard and made it plain to himself that those boys were the chief cause of his trouble.

"I'm sure I don't know," he said sadly, "I never did

anything to make them hate me, that I can think of. I spoiled their putting pepper on the stove that time, you know, but I don't see as that was any reason for hating me; then, after they shut me in the cellar and got found out, they were worse than ever, though I wasn't to blame for that, anyhow. I didn't know who shut the door."

"They hated me without a cause," said Mrs. Selsmer gravely. "I found that verse in our big Bible today. It is one of Grandmother's too; it was marked all around. I don't know why she chose it, unless she wanted to remember who had to suffer in that way for her sake. You know who it was, don't you, Ralph?"

"Jesus," said the boy reverently. "Mother, it must have been hard to bear; and He had false witnesses, too. So have I, if they say they saw me do the stealing. I never felt, before, how dreadful it must have been for Him to have stood there and heard such lies told. Mother, do you suppose they will be able to make up a story about me that shall sound like the truth?"

"I don't know," said Mrs. Selmser; "the other false witnesses didn't. They couldn't agree, you know; it is hard for false witnesses to agree in just the right things, and make no mistakes."

"I guess I'll take that for my verse," Ralph said, after a thoughtful pause, "that one you found, Mother; it is true enough of me, and it will make me think, maybe—" Here he came to an abrupt pause; he was not used to speaking out all his feelings. What he thought was, that maybe the verse would remind him how much harder were Jesus' sufferings than his own.

That evening Dr. Welborne returned, and the next

day, which was Saturday, set about finding out what he could of the trouble. He kept his own counsel, so far at least as the scholars were concerned, but something that he found took him in search of two boys—the very boys who had been the means of Ralph's spending some unhappy hours in the schoolhouse cellar. They were engaged in a game of tag with a dozen or so of the village boys. Jimmie Bostwick was one of the runners, so Dr. Welborne decided to wait for him a while, but his friend Harry West stood looking on, with his hands in his pockets. Him Dr. Welborne summoned to come at once to his study on special business.

Arriving there, Dr. Welborne, without more delay, having told Harry that he had been informed he was the one who had seen Ralph Selsmer taking papers from the desk, asked two or three rapid questions.

"What time of day was it when you saw this done?"

Now this was one of the questions which Harry had not planned for. At first he did not know what to say, but Dr. Welborne's eyes were on him, and he must say something, so he answered that it was about noon.

"Are you sure of that?"

"Yes, sir," said Harry; "quite sure."

"What leads you to be sure of that?"

Another troublesome question, but Harry had been caught in places before where he had to invent reasons for things, so, after a moments thought, he was ready.

"Why, sir, I heard the twelve o'clock bell ring, and I whispered to Jimmie that the thief would get a licking for being late to dinner."

"Ah," said Dr. Welborne, "then you and Jimmie

were near enough together to whisper about it, were you?"

"Yes, sir."

"That will do for the present," said the doctor. "You may take a seat over there by the library table, and interest yourself in any books you please. I shall wish you to remain here for the afternoon."

Harry looked dismayed. There were reasons why he wanted to get out and see his friend Jimmie, at once.

"If you please, sir," he said hesitating, "I'm afraid my mother will be very much troubled. She wanted me to be sure and come home at three o'clock to drive her to the train to meet my father. He is coming from the city on the three o'clock train, and will expect me to be there."

"Indeed!" said Dr. Welborne. "If that is the case I will tell my man, who has just driven to the door with my carriage, that he may take a message from me to your mother, and offer his services to do your work, because I shall need you to stay here."

Now when I tell you that Harry's mother did not expect him at all, and that his father was not away from home, and that Dr. Welborne had met him and had a few minutes' talk with him only an hour before, you will understand why the boy felt much dismayed, and why Dr. Welborne said to himself, "If all his statements are as trustworthy as this, we shall get on rapidly."

However, he sent his man not only to do that unnecessary errand, but to drive to the woods where the boys were playing, and bring James Bostwick to him without delay.

When James, large-eyed and trembling, arrived, Dr. Welborne coolly turned the key on Harry, and went with his other witness to a room across the hall. There, after several other questions had been asked and answered, came this one: "What time of day was it when you saw those papers taken?"

"It was about, let me see—oh! I know, sir, it must have been between five and six o'clock?"

"Why must it have been that time?"

"Because I remember it was getting dark very fast; and I thought to myself that I should miss the five o'clock car as sure as the world, and have to foot it home; and I did."

"Then you are quite sure, of course, that it could not have been, say, about noon?"

"Oh! yes, sir, indeed I am. I was not in town at noon. I went into the city with Father, and came home on the three o'clock train."

"Ah!" said Dr. Welborne again. He happened to know that Jimmie, on the day in question, was in town all day long, and so was his father.

"Did you and Harry have any communication while you were hidden behind the screen? Were you near enough together to whisper?"

"No, sir, we were not. I was at one end of the long screen and he at the other; we couldn't have spoken without Ralph's hearing us."

"Very well. I have all the information I desire for the present; but I shall have to ask you to take a seat and wait for me here, as I shall want to see you again presently."

Whereupon the key turned on Jimmie, and Dr. Welborne went to his upstairs study, where by this time young Sherman Barwood had been summoned to see him.

It is a long, sad story. I am sure you do not care to hear the weary particulars of evil doers.

Neither do I imagine you will be greatly surprised to learn that Sherman Barwood, with the help of these two young tools of his, had planned and carried out the whole wicked thing. It took some time to get all the tangle of sin and falsehood unraveled, but Dr. Welborne was patient, and determined; and because of the fact that the two principal witnesses, in the course of ten-minutes talk with him, had told three falsehoods, was convinced that they would be quite capable of telling others. On the other hand, the only suspicious thing about Ralph Selsmer was, he had of late been intimate with Sherman Barwood, a boy whom Dr. Welborne did not trust; and he remembered that "evil communications corrupt good manners".

It was a very hard lesson for Ralph Selsmer, but I think he learned a great deal from it.

"Neither so did their witness agree together," quoted his mother solemnly, when Ralph told the story at home, and explained how Dr. Welborne had gotten his clue.

Ralph was struck with the verse, it so exactly fitted his own case. He found it in Grandmother's Bible, and sat for some time thinking about it. Thinking also over these questions: Had he, during this trial, acted at all as Jesus would have done in his place? Did he ever act much like Jesus at any time?

# CHAPTER IX.

*Then Samuel answered, speak, for thy servant heareth.*

*His sons made themselves vile.*

*Cease to do evil; learn to do well.*

*Nevertheless, the people refused to obey the voice of Samuel; and they said, Nay, but we will have a king over us.*

Whatever may have been said of the rest of the world on the Fourth of July afternoon, Ned Selmser was happy. No soldier of the Revolution ever rode to victory and honor more proudly than he pranced up and down the floor of the best room on his wooden horse.

Somebody had fished it out of the attic—a bruised and battered charger long past it's prime—and sent it to Ned the day before, thereby making him royally happy.

He and Mother were alone together, which was another cause for pleasure. Ned was very fond of his mother, and she was a busy woman. On this afternoon, though she sewed, she did not do it with the air of haste that belonged to common days. In fact her work often lay idly in her lap while she watched Ned and chatted with him. She even undertook to answer all his questions, a task which was at all times hard.

The day was warm. Ned and his mother wore as few clothes as would at all do, and made themselves in every way as comfortable as they could, because it was the Fourth of July.

Into the quiet of this home scene presently burst Ralph, his face red with violent running, his hair blown into wild disorder, his hands blackened with powder and

soot, his eyes big with terror, and his voice loud: "Mother, oh, Mother! They want you to go down to

Smith's right away; little Jim is burned to death, I guess; he's awfully hurt, anyhow!"

Before this sentence was finished, Mrs. Selmser had dropped her work, shaken down her sleeves, which had been tucked up for coolness, seized a bonnet from the drawer near at hand, and was jerking it hastily into place while she asked questions.

"How did it happen, Ralph? Who told you? Is anybody there? Have they gone for the doctor?"

"The cannon," said Ralph, sitting down in the doorway, and fanning himself with his hat; "it exploded, or something, just as they were ready to fire it off, made an awful noise, and little Jim, who was close to it, fell just as though he had been shot, and clapped his hands to his eyes and gave one dreadful scream and then lay still."

Ralph shuddered while he spoke. The sight of little Jim had evidently frightened him.

Mrs. Selmser was in a great hurry. By this time she was two steps down the walk, but she stopped long enough to ask one more question: "Ralph, how do you know all these things?"

Whereat, Ralph's face grew redder than before; but his mother did not wait for the answer. It was a miserable afternoon, especially to little Ned, who found Ralph a very poor substitute for his mother.

It seemed to him that supper time would never come; but it did, and with it the various members of the family.

Mrs. Selmser did most of the talking; she had many things to tell about the accident.

Little Jim was badly hurt. The doctor feared his

eyes were ruined, and there was also a grave doubt about his ever being able to walk any more.

Mrs. Selmser told how brave he was, and how he had made them all cry by trying to explain to his mother that his big brother was not to blame for his getting hurt. It was not until the supper, which was especially nice on account of its being the Fourth of July, was almost eaten, that Mr. Selmser turned suddenly to Ralph.

"Now, my boy, it is time to understand another part of this afternoon's work. How happens it that you were on hand to see and hear all this, and to be the first to run for help?"

Ralph dropped his head almost to his plate, and muttered so low that, although it was very still, he could hardly be understood.

"Speak up, my boy," said his father. "If you have anything to say, say it so your mother and I can hear. Were you on the hill where the cannon was fired?"

"Yes, sir," said Ralph, his head still dropped.

"How did that happen? Were you sent there on duty by someone who had a right to send you?"

"No sir."

"Did you forget my orders, that you were on no account to go in the direction of the cannon today?"

"No, sir." Ralph's voice kept getting lower and lower, still he could be heard. His replies sounded miserably short and mean, even to himself; but there was nothing to add to them, that he could think of.

"Well," said his father, after a pause, "have you anything more to say?"

Then Ralph raised his head and spoke hurriedly. "I

didn't mean to go, Father; I was standing away down below, looking in that direction, and I saw something strange that I couldn't make out, and I went a little nearer just to see what it was. Then one of the boys wanted me to go up and see the cannon's great big mouth; he said they weren't going to fire the cannon for an hour yet, so I went; I thought you wouldn't care if I went to look at it, and came away before it was fired; and I stayed longer than I meant to, but not nearly an hour. Then I found they were getting ready to fire, and I thought you wouldn't like me to be running down the hill while the cannon was going off. I meant to go the first minute I could, sir; and then came the accident, and I was the first to see little Jim drop; so I ran for his father, and then home to Mother."

It sounded like a very weak story. Ralph could not help thinking so; he thought so the more because his father was quite silent. He thought so still more when his father said at last with a sigh, "I am sorry to hear your story, my son. I had hoped you had some excuse for your disobedience, or some explanation beyond the fact that you wanted to do what you had been forbidden, and so did it; but it seems you have not."

Now Ralph had meant that his story should excuse his conduct. It was humiliating to think he had so utterly failed.

Mr. Selmser sighed again before he spoke.

"I am very sorry for you, my son; it seems to me that one explosion of a cannon is a good deal to pay for all that must follow. The fireworks will be very fine tonight, and I have been at some pains and some expense to provide a good place for us all to see them; but you have counted yourself out. You will go to your room at eight o'clock, and go to bed. Tomorrow I will talk further with you about this thing and see what can be done."

To say that Ralph was dismayed, will hardly express the feeling he had. He was utterly dumbfounded! As a rule, he was a boy who obeyed. He was not used to being punished; he had so fully meant to obey today, that he can hardly be said to have realized that his act was deliberate disobedience. He had argued that his father's reason for not wanting him to go on the hill where the cannon was to be fired, was because he feared he would be hurt. A foolish fear, Ralph thought, but nevertheless such was the reason; now of course if he did not stay until time for firing the cannon, he could not possibly get hurt; and equally of course if they fired the cannon before the time, it was not his fault. This is the way he had reasoned it out in the afternoon, while he was being cross to Ned; and this is what he had tried to explain, but some way it wouldn't explain very well. He had expected that his father would disapprove, and would perhaps speak sharply to him, and say that he thought he could trust him better than that; but the idea that he would be forbidden to see the fireworks had not so much as entered his mind! Why, there had never been such a display of fireworks in the town as there was to be tonight, and from his very babyhood Ralph had been wild after fireworks and powder and cannon, and everything of that sort. It seemed too terrible to be borne that he, Ralph Selmser, a boy unused to punishment, was to be sent to bed at eight o'clock on that evening of all evenings in the year! And all because he had gone up the hill for a few minutes, to see the cannon before it was fired. It was unjust, cruel! These things he thought, but wisely did not say. He was well enough acquainted with his father to know that there was no use in his saying anything.

By eight o'clock Ralph and his mother were alone. She had declined to go to see the fireworks, though Ralph knew that she had meant to go, and lost her interest on his account. He muttered to himself that Father had ruined her evening as well as his, and felt very sullen indeed.

It is a wonder, in this frame of mind, he should have given any attention to the big old Bible, but the habit of looking out a verse before he went to bed was so strong upon him, that he drew it to him, and turned the leaves listlessly, stopping before the first marked verse which caught his eye: "His sons made themselves vile and he restrained them not." Why, here was a surprising thing. He had been all the evening blaming his father in his heart for "restraining" him, and had fallen in with a Bible story where the father displeased the Lord because he did not restrain his sons. Ralph read backward and forward, until he had the story; until his heart was tender toward old Eli for the suffering which he had brought on himself and his sons.

"He couldn't bear to do it, I s'pose," he said, half aloud. He was thinking about Eli, but his mother thought he was speaking of his father.

"No, he couldn't; he said if he could stay at home for you from every sight there would be to see for a year, and have that do as well, he would jump at the chance. But he knew that it wouldn't be doing his duty by you to let things go." No answer from Ralph. In his heart he thought, with a touch of pride, "My father is a stronger man than Eli was."

The distant lights of the Roman candles were visible in the sky when Ralph went to bed, but as he looked at them he said to himself, "I suppose I've got a father to be proud of. If there were to be a new Bible written, it would never say such a thing about him as it did about poor old Eli. And there's another thing; there shouldn't be anything in there about me that was anything like Eli's sons. I suppose they began by going to look at 'great big mouths', or something, not meaning to do anything worse. I've begun but I'll stop right here. I'll tell Father so tomorrow morning, and say 'thank you' besides, see if I don't!"

# CHAPTER X.

*By me kings reign, and princes decree justice.*
*Only fear the Lord and serve him in truth with all*
*your heart; for consider how great things he*
*hath done for you.*
*Because thou hast rejected the word of the Lord, he*
*hath also rejected thee from being king.*
*Man looketh on the outward appearance, but the*
*Lord looketh on the heart.*

It would be difficult to explain to thoughtless people
what there had been in Ralph's day to give him such
grave and humble thoughts as he had that evening.

In some respects it had been a remarkable day. In
the first place, there had been a tremendous shower—the
hardest Ralph ever remembered to have seen and heard.
I think the grave thoughts began with that, perhaps.
Ralph was not the sort of boy who could frolic and giggle
through a thunderstorm; he had sense enough to
understand that there was something solemn about it,
which ought to make people think. After the storm, little
Harvey Briggs, who lived down near Pemberton Square,
escaped from his mother's eye, for she was a
washerwoman and had to keep her eyes very busy, and
went to have a frolic on his own account in the little
rivers which the storm had made directly along the
roadside.

A most charming time was Harvey having,

imagining himself to have been shipwrecked in mid-ocean, with nothing but his own skill and wisdom to save him from drowning. Meantime, there was real danger just behind him. A man had been climbing a ladder to fix something on the roof of the great building; he had just reached the ground again, when something up above got out of place, swung around, hit the ladder, swaying it to one side, sending it in the direction where little Harvey played. "Look out there!" shouted the man. And a dozen men "looked out", and looked around, but little Harvey did not; he was used to a great deal of noise on the Square. Somebody told someone else to "look out!" every few minutes; they never meant him. It was all done in a second of time, of course; it doesn't take a ladder long to fall. The men were all several feet away from Harvey, but Ralph Selmser was not; he was almost at the boy's side when the shout came. He was quick-witted: a long step, a quick jerk with his strong young arm, and there was a ladder lying just where Harvey had played, and an enraged boy kicking and screaming because his playing had been interrupted; and a shout of praise from the crowd who had already gathered, over the promptness of the boy Ralph. "You saved the young scamp's life," one man said, shaking his head at the angry little boy; and Ralph, looking at the ladder, lying just where Harvey's foot had left an impression in the mud, believed he had.

It seemed astonishing to him that not two hours afterward he should meet a horse running away, with two ignorant boys doing what they could to make it run still faster, in the vain hope of stopping it. In the little buggy, almost paralyzed with fear, was seated Nellie Rives, the niece of Colonel Rives, on Marchmont Street. Ralph knew the horse; knew that angry as he looked, he could be easily managed. The horse was dashing straight toward him; he stood perfectly still in the path, and at the right moment made a spring for the bridle, at the same time calling the horse by name and speaking in the most assured and soothing tone imaginable. In almost less time than it takes me to tell it, the horse was moving along at a respectable pace, and Ralph was seated beside Nellie, with the reins in his hand, she being too frightened to do any more driving.

On the whole, it had certainly been a day to remember. Ralph had been talked about, and praised, and rewarded, until his mother said, with a loving smile, it would not be much wonder if he became as "vain as a peacock". Ralph's mother was one of those who felt very proud of him.

Yet, despite it all—rather, because of it all—the boy sat, at about eight o'clock, with his eyes fixed on the big Bible, with his chin leaning on his hand, and his face, as I said, very grave. The marked verse which attracted him was this: "Man looketh on the outward appearance, but the Lord looketh on the heart."

"It's as true as the world!" said Ralph to himself. "All that people see of me is the outside. They think I'm brave, and thoughtful, and good-hearted, and all that, and say I will make a man to be proud of. How do they know? What do they know about me, anyhow? It didn't take much bravery to jerk little Harvey from under the ladder; I knew I could skip before it would tumble. It took more of—something or other, whatever the name of it is—to keep from shaking the little scamp for bawling so loud because I wouldn't give him a chance to kill himself. Then there was that horse! Who would think of being afraid of old Gray Rives? He wouldn't have jumped half so high if those simpletons who were trying to stop him hadn't scared him so with their caps and their yells. I knew I could stop him; anybody could, who was worth a cent and a half. It is all the 'outward appearance,' just as the verse says. Now I know I'm not near so good a boy as folks think. And what is more, the Lord knows it, too. He "looketh on the heart". Then He sees that I'm not serving Him the way I know I ought; in the way I promised to do. I'm a coward instead of a brave boy; that's what I am. I'm not afraid of a tumbling ladder that can't touch me, nor a horse that I've known all my life, most; but I'm afraid to come out squarely and say I'm a soldier of Jesus Christ, and stick to it, times when somebody might laugh. I said I would, and I meant to, but I don't do it; and the reason is, I'm a coward. Mother doesn't know it, and there doesn't anybody know it except just the Lord, and Ralph Selmser. The 'outward appearance' is pretty near right with me most of the time, though once in a while, it seems, when the temptation is big, as it was the Fourth of July, for instance, why, I get even the 'outward appearance' wrong. The fact is, I need to be brave enough to say, 'Boys, that's wrong,' when those two boys in our grade use coarse words, and tell mean stories. I need to be brave enough to walk off the other way, when Arthur Brooks asks me to walk with him, and swears a little every few minutes. If I am a soldier of the Lord Jesus Christ—and I really believe I am—He must be ashamed of me about half the time; and here the folks all over town are calling me brave! As sure as the world, it is time for me to turn over a new leaf. I'm going in for heart bravery from this very night. There's lots of places where it looks all right outside, and where I know inside it's wrong, and the outside has had it, so far as I'm concerned, a great deal of the time. More shame to me, with Grandmother's Bible to depend on all the while!

"Ralph Selmser, more than twenty men have told you today that you were a brave boy, and had reason to be proud of your record; and you know perfectly well that in the sense it ought to be, it isn't true. Don't let you and me ever have to own that again as long as we live."

He was in his room alone while all this earnest thinking was going on. He rose up, presently, closed the big Bible with a reverent hand, and got down on his knees.

If I had been his mother I should have been proud of him then.

# CHAPTER XI.

*If God be for us, who can be against us?*
*There is a friend that sticketh closer than a*
*    brother.*
*Be not overcome with evil, but overcome evil with*
*    good.*
*The face of the Lord is against them that do evil.*

Over that verse, "Be not overcome with evil, but
overcome evil with good," Ralph Selmser paused
thoughtfully. What a grand thing it would be to do that.

He had enemies, you will remember, and they were
by no means more sweetly disposed toward him because
they had been discovered in their sin and punishment.
Ralph had very little to do with them nowadays.

But as he read the verse he said to himself he should
just like a chance of doing something splendid for them.
Suppose he should have a fortune of a hundred thousand
dollars left to him, he would give them each a thousand
the first thing he did. That would be "overcoming evil
with good" in a splendid fashion! But then he
recollected mournfully that there was not the least hope
of his having a chance to do such a fine thing. "Nor
anything else," he said, with a grave shake of his head, as
he closed the big old Bible.

"There are no caves, nowadays, where I could find
a fellow and cut off a piece of his coat." He had been
reading that fascinating story of David finding Saul in the

cave, and cutting off a piece of his robe, but saving his life. Ralph admired David very much, and was sure he would like nothing better than to have a chance of that sort come to him.

He thought about it several times the next day, probably because he had chosen the verse I have quoted for his own; but because it was such an unlikely thing that he should ever have a chance to do any great favors to his enemies the verse gradually faded from his mind, until one evening on his way home something happened which brought it before him again.

It was vacation, and he seldom saw the boys who had given him so much trouble. One of them he knew was working for Farmer Stevens, and working hard. The fact was, Farmer Stevens had a hard name among them.

"He isn't what you can call cruel," Ned Porter explained, "but he is most uncommon cross; he's well enough when things go just right, and he gives you enough to eat, and all that, but he thinks a boy ought never to forget, or to be late in the morning, or late at night, or to be anything else but perfect; and the way he scolds you if you forget one of the chores, or do not shut a gate, or open it at just the right minute, is a caution! He can do more than scold, too, I can tell you!" Ned had worked one whole summer for Farmer Stevens, and knew what he was talking about.

Much of what had been told him came freshly to Ralph's mind on this same evening, as he sauntered home with his basket full of berries. He had tramped about three miles in search of nice ones, and was moving slowly to enjoy the cool air after his afternoon's work.

When, in crossing the meadow which lay between him and the village, he came plump upon the oldest and most disagreeable of his enemies stretched at full length on the long grass, fast asleep. Ralph stopped short. He had met Brindle and Dolly, two of Farmer Stevens' choicest cows, moving leisurely across the meadow on the other side of the creek, as he came across, and wondered why they were not at home being milked. Now he understood the situation. Brindle and Dolly were this sleeper's special care; it was his duty to see that they came home at a certain moment, through a certain choice field, the gate of which was always kept locked, lest some careless boy or man should leave it open, and the key of which at this moment lay on the grass beside the dreamer.

What a scolding he would get if the two choice cows wandered away and could not be found for hours. Suppose they should get in somewhere where they ought not, and do mischief! Ralph felt pretty sure that the "something else" which Ned told about with that shrug of his shoulders, would be forthcoming under such circumstances. "Serve him right, too," he muttered. "What business has a boy to go to sleep like a baby, in broad daylight?"

Then there came to him the sound of that verse of his, and the memory of the sleeper in the cave, with his enemy bending over him.

A smile shone all over Ralph's roguish face as he thought what a thing it would be to cut a bit from this sleeper's torn pocket, to prove to him who had stood beside him!

He had no idea of doing it; he had sense enough to know that times were greatly changed since David's day, and that the circumstances were very different; but as plainly as though somebody had told him, he knew what he might do. He was going directly past the gate where the cows ought to turn in; a walk of five minutes out of his direct road would take him past the very barnyard where they were being waited for. What if he should take the cows along with him? Was it likely the boy would get into trouble if the cows were at home all right? Of course he wouldn't sleep long, boys never did; he might waken him, to be sure, but that he could not bring himself to do. The boy was so much larger than he, was so angry at him, and had made such ugly threats as to what he would do if he ever caught Ralph alone anywhere, that Ralph, though no coward, felt that he would much rather deal with the cows than the boy. He hesitated, but only for a moment. This was not a cave, it was true, and he felt no desire to take his enemy's life, and he knew it was not a very wonderful thing to do for him; yet it was a possible chance of saving him from punishment.

Ralph resolved to try it, so picking up the padlock key he made his way across the meadow to where he had seen the cows; there they were, close to the fence. They seemed astonished to see Ralph, but they followed him willingly enough, especially after he had unlocked the gate and let them through the field with which they were acquainted. They tried to nibble a few things that they ought not to touch, but finding Ralph resolute, gave it up, and marched dignifiedly through. It was a little later than usual, certainly, and Ralph was wondering just what he should say, supposing he should see Farmer Stevens, and he asked about the missing boy when he reached the barnyard where the cows belonged. It was deserted, save for the kitten, who frolicked about the old tub, which had evidently been set out for Brindle and Dolly. This was fortunate for Ralph. He had often been in this yard visiting Ned Porter, and Farmer Stevens had rigid rules about keys and everything else, so the key hung in its place, and he made all speed out of the yard toward home. Just as he turned the corner which led him past Farmer Stevens' kitchen door, he heard a voice ask, "Where's the boy?" And another answer, "I don't know, he can't be far away. The cows are here all right, and the key is in its place. I suppose he's attending to his chores."

"I suppose he's asleep," said Ralph gleefully to himself, as he stepped briskly homeward.

It would be very nice if I could finish this story by telling you that the sleepy boy found out who had befriended him and come to thank him with tears of gratitude in his eyes, and was his friend forever after. But nothing of the kind happened. He was astonished and frightened when he awoke, to discover how late it was, and that the key was gone. He wasted some precious moments looking for it, and was so frightened because he could not find it that he could hardly get home. He was so astonished, when he reached there, to find that the cows were in their place, and so was the key, and that nobody seemed to know that he had been late, he did not know what to think. He puzzled over the strange experience a great deal, but nothing like the truth came to him. To this day he does not know how the cows reached home, and how the key contrived to hang itself where it belonged.

You think, therefore, that Ralph had no reward for his kindness? In that you are mistaken. He felt so pleased whenever he thought of it that he got happiness enough out of it for some days. More than that, he found, to his great surprise, that he did not feel bitter toward the boy any more. The fact that he had done him a kindness seemed to have soothed his ruffled feelings a great deal.

In short, he made a discovery which will be worth a great deal to him in life: that if you really want to forgive an enemy, and feel as though you couldn't, all you need to do is to hunt about for some way in which to give him a lift, and the "forgiving" will creep in of itself.

# CHAPTER XII.

Behold how good and how pleasant it is for brethren
    to dwell together in unity.
The Lord loveth the gates of Zion more than all the
    dwellings of Jacob.
In everything give thanks; for this is the will of God
    in Christ Jesus, concerning you.
Therefore being justified by faith, we have peace
    with God, through our Lord Jesus Christ.

If it had not been for the picture I do not know that
it would have happened at all. Ralph did not feel in the
least like reading. In fact he had been too much
interested in the talk between his father and mother to
forget it easily, or to turn his mind to any other subject.

The fact is, the Selmsers—since times had changed
with them for the better—had been looking about for a
home. That is, they looked about for a piece of land on
which they might sometime, away in the years to come,
build a little house which should be their very own.
"And no rent to pay," said Ralph aloud, using the words
almost with an awe, when he first heard them. Ever
since he could remember, the quarter's rent had to be
planned for with as much care, oh! with a great deal more
care, than the next day's dinner. Sometimes it had been
very hard work indeed to raise the required sum; Ralph
had known of almost sleepless nights and anxious days

concerning it. To be free from the burden of rent seemed almost to him like having wings.

"But it is a long way ahead, Ralph," the Mother would say, smiling at first, then sighing a little. She would have liked a home very much.

Within the past few weeks much exciting talk had been going on in the Selmser home about this very matter. It happened that a neat little house stood on a bit of land, which had been the desire of Mr. Selmser's heart ever since he had seriously thought about the possibility of a home of his own. It happened also that, very unexpectedly, the house and the land were offered for sale—offered on remarkably easy terms. The owner's wife had died, and the owner and his boys were restless, and wanted to go away off to California, or somewhere, to see if they would be less desolate without "mother".

"All he wants down is five hundred dollars," said Mr. Selmser, repeating the sentence for the third time. "The rest can lie as long as anybody wants it to—as long as I liked, he said to me. He says he would rather have us on the old place than anybody he knows, because it would seem more homelike to think of it; that you knew his wife so well, and was so kind to her in her sickness."

"Poor man!" said Mrs. Selmser.

"He says," continued Mr. Selmser, after a pause, in which he had looked sorrowful, in sympathy with his neighbor's sorrow, "if he could manage to get along with less cash he would, for the sake of letting me have it; but he thinks he must raise that amount on it, in order to meet his expenses; and it is reasonable that he should. I told him so. I told him that I couldn't expect him to offer for less money down; but that, at the same time, he might as well say a thousand as five hundred, as far as we are concerned. I told him that with all our efforts—and you doing wonders to help along and the children too—the very utmost that we had been able to save toward a home had been two hundred in cash, and that it would be likely to be a good many years before we would have one at that rate, for such an offer as his didn't start up everyday. He wanted to know if your sister's folks couldn't advance a little money for us."

Mrs. Selmser shook her head and sewed faster than ever.

"So I told him," said Mr. Selmser, after a thoughtful pause. "I said we had never borrowed, even when at our worst, and we couldn't think of doing it now; and we wouldn't want to borrow of them, anyway, because—"

"Well," said Mr. Selmser, after interrupting himself and being silent for a minute, "there's no use in going into that; of course I didn't tell him any reasons. He thinks the head of our firm would lend it to me, and I haven't much doubt but that he would, if he were here himself; but I told Brooks that he wouldn't be at home for five or six months, and then I don't know as we would like to borrow, anyhow."

"No," said Mrs. Selmser emphatically. "Oh, no! Don't let us do that; we didn't, as you say, at the worst, and we don't want to begin."

"Well," Mr. Selmser had said, pushing back his chair at last, and rising, "I've got to go around to the warehouse to look after some freight, and I may be hindered for an hour or two. So you see we will have to plan for the rent this good while yet; eh, Mother?"

He spoke exactly as though the hindering freight was what was keeping them from getting rid of the rent; but Mrs. Selmser knew that he was simply fitting the last part of the sentence to the subject which had been in their thoughts so long, and she looked up and smiled.

"We can do it," she said pleasantly, and her husband went away with her kind voice and smile in his thoughts. As he closed the door he sighed and said, "Poor Brooks!" It was impossible not to contrast his own pleasant home with the desolate one around the corner.

It was just after this talk that Ralph, reminded by his mother that it was growing late, drew the large Bible toward him and began to turn the leaves in a listless way, his mind still on the house he wished they had. As he turned he came upon a picture. Not a photograph, nor an engraving, but a pencil sketch, very neatly and carefully finished, of a pretty girl in an old-fashioned dress, with short waist and puffed sleeves, seated in an old-fashioned rope swing.

"Why, Mother," he said, "here is a picture of a girl in a swing in Grandmother's Bible!"

Mrs. Selmser made an exclamation of surprise and delight at this, and looked over his shoulder.

"I want to know!" she said. "I do wonder if you have found that picture. I'm as glad, Ralph, as though it was a fifty dollar bill—I don't know but I'm more glad. That's all the picture I ever had of my dear old mother."

"Of your mother!" Ralph repeated in amazement; "that was never Grandmother's picture!"

"Yes, it was; and very much like her, too, every one said. My own grandmother used to tell me about it by the hour. 'It was as like two peas in a pod,' she said. A real, genuine artist took it—a portrait painter he was. Grandfather—my grandfather, that is—would have liked to get Mother painted, but he couldn't afford that, so the artist, who was boarding at his house and sketching in the neighborhood, made this pencil picture for her because she showed him the way to the pond where the largest lilies were to be found. Mother gave it to me once, but your Aunt Maria wanted it dreadfully to frame, she said, so I gave it to her, but she never framed it and after awhile she lost it. She hunted everywhere for it; we all did, after Mother was gone, but we couldn't find it, and here it is shut up in Grandmother's Bible! Dear heart! I believe she took care of it herself and saved it for me; she meant me to have the Bible, always. I shall not part with it again, I know that. Mother was a very pretty girl, everybody said," and she looked long and tenderly at the pretty young face that Ralph remembered only in cap and spectacles.

"Perhaps Grandmother saved other things for you in the big old Bible," said Ralph, turning the leaves slowly. He was more interested in that thought than he was in the little-girl picture of his grandmother, but his mother's eyes, now filled with tears, were on the pictured face, and she only answered dreamily, "Maybe so," as Ralph turned the leaves.

She was still studying the picture when his next exclamation startled her. "Mother, here are two leaves stuck together. Why, they are pasted together, I do believe; look! All along that under edge, and along the side, they stick just as close! I can't get them apart."

It was certainly so; and now Mrs. Selmser was as much excited as Ralph; what if she should find a letter from that dear mother to herself, or to one of her children! The leaves at the top were found to be free, the bottom and sides having been pasted together, thus forming a neat little bag for a paper of some sort which was certainly lying inside. Ralph drew it forth with a grave face and a reverent hand, and read to his mother the words on the outside.

They were these: "In everything give thanks, for this is the will of God in Christ Jesus, concerning you."

"Precious Mother," murmured Mrs. Selmser, reaching out her hand for the paper. "That is just like her; her last will, Ralph, to you and me. Let us always do it; don't let us ever fret or worry about anything; just give thanks for our blessings."

She was wiping away the tears as she spoke, that she might be better able to see her mother's handwriting.

"There's something inside," said Ralph, and they unfolded the outer paper. This also Ralph read:

"For whoever in my daughter Jane's family shall find it first."

"That's you," said Mrs. Selmser, with a kind of solemn joy in her face. "Oh, Ralph! My boy, you've got something of your very own, from the best grandmother who ever lived."

Ralph's face was pale; there was something solemn and beautiful about this gift, whatever it was. His hand trembled so he could hardly open the paper which enclosed it. One, two, three, four, five, six bank bills, and everyone of them representing fifty dollars! As Ralph took in this astounding fact, his face from being quite pale, suddenly glowed a deep crimson. "Mother," he said, "oh, Mother, only think! There are three hundred dollars here."

What they said, and what they did, and how they managed to endure their excitement until first Sarah Jane and then the Father came home, I have not time to tell; nor, indeed, what those two said and did to add to the excitement after they came. Just one bit more I must give you.

Ralph, who had been silent for about two minutes, suddenly said aloud, "Three and two are five. Hurray! I know what we'll do. There's the five hundred— your two and my three make five. We'll buy the house, we will, as sure as beans! Father, I hate rent!"

# A Hedge Fence

by

Isabella Alden

1884

# Contents

# Chapter I.

*And when he had spoken these things, while they*
*beheld, he was taken up.*
*And they were all filled with the Holy Ghost.*
*Then they that gladly received his word were*
*baptized.*
*Then shall the lame man leap as an hart, and the*
*tongue of the dumb sing.*

*Cooledge, Jan., 18—*

Dear Renie:

Was I to write the first letter ? I can't remember.
Mother says it makes no difference, but I think it does;
because, you see, the first fellow is ahead all the time,
and always has to write next. This is a real jolly country.
We went to the State House the other day, and saw the
Governor. He spoke to us, shook hands, and said he used
to be a boy himself once. Folks say he was a good boy.
I asked Father if governors were always good boys, and
he laughed, and said if they were, some of them changed
a great deal when they got to be men.

I've got something funny to tell you. The other day
we got into an awful scrape, Tim and I. We didn't mean
to, either of us. He didn't think, and I forgot, and that

was all there was about it. That is, about the beginning of it; before it ended, there was a good deal. I did mean to tell you all about it, but I guess I won't. It is past now, and I'd kind of like to forget it. But I'll tell you something that came of it. Mr. Harris Browning was here. You don't know him, but you ought to; everybody ought to know him, I guess, especially boys. He likes boys first-rate, and he is always doing something nice for them. He is awful good too. He was spending a week here, visiting the Truesdale folks—they are our boarders. Well, I sat in the dining-room studying my lesson. I was all alone. Tim was upstairs studying his lesson. We couldn't be together because of that scrape I told you of. I felt lonesome and bad. I was thinking, and I spoke out loud. Says I:

"If there was some kind of a hedge to keep a fellow inside of things so he needn't forever be tumbling out and getting into scrapes, I'd like it." Just then in came Mr. Harris Browning. It was raining, and he had been out in the rain and had a dripping umbrella, and he came through the dining room to put it in a safe place. Then he came back and stood by the table and looked at me.

"What's that, my boy?" he said; and I told him what it was. "A hedge," he said, and he laughed a little. "What sort of a hedge? A fence? And how high would it have to be so that you couldn't climb over?"

"I wouldn't try to climb," I said; "or if I forgot and began to climb it, it would give me a prick, and that would make me think, and I'd jump back. A fellow is always getting into scrapes because he doesn't have time to think, and that would give him time."

"I see," he said. "It isn't a bad idea. Well now, my friend, I think I can help you about that. Suppose I send a hedge to you, a new one each month, or a new piece of one, and you can put them together yourself. I think I can manage a piece of one that will give you a prick whenever you try to climb."

"Send it!" I said. "Send a hedge! How would you go to work to do it?"

"That's my part of the bargain," he said, and he laughed again. "I'll agree to furnish the hedge if you'll agree to take care of it. Set it up in its proper place, and see that it has a chance to help you. A hedge set up over in the ten-acre lot wouldn't help keep you inside this yard, you know."

Well, we had some more talk, and the next morning he went away. And the very next afternoon came a card by mail for me, and it had all these verses that I put at the top of my letter, and a cute little hedge. The letters were woven into each other in the cutest kind of way, making a regular hedge fence all around a fellow who stood in the corner, who I suppose was me. I thought it was a pretty thing enough, but I didn't see what help it could be. But I put it in my pocket, and what do you think happened the next evening? First, though, about the fence. There was a cute little hand pointing to something at the end of that first verse, and I looked to see where it pointed, and it said: Acts 1:2. So I got Mother's Bible and looked at it, and that said: "Ye men of Galilee, why stand ye gazing up into heaven? This same Jesus, which is taken up from you into heaven, shall so come in like manner as ye have seen him go into heaven."

Well, it was a nice evening; the sky was just as blue as it could be, and there were ten thousand million stars twinkling. But I felt awful lonesome and gloomy. Tim had gone home to stay a week, and Mother hadn't come. She had been gone two weeks, and I'd been with Father to the depot to meet her, and she wasn't there. Now when a fellow's mother doesn't come, maybe you know how it feels. I didn't want to go in the house a bit. I knew Father would read the paper, and look gloomy, because he didn't like Mother's not coming a bit more than I did; and then he would write letters—and Tim was gone, and I didn't know what to do. I had been to the telegraph office for one of the boarders, and I hung on the gate and wished I didn't have to go in the house.

Just then Jerry Davis came along. He isn't the best kind of a boy, but he is pleasant enough. He stopped when he saw me.

"Good luck," he said. "I was hoping I'd find you outdoors. Come on down to the mill-pond. The ice is prime, and we'll have a skate and a race."

Well, sir, I wanted to go like anything! It was such a nice night, and I hadn't been to the pond this winter. I knew Father wouldn't miss me, because of the papers and the letters, and Mother wasn't at home to worry. She didn't like to have me go to the pond when she was at home, because it worried her; and I knew Father wouldn't let me go if I asked him; but Mother being away I pretty near made up my mind to go; but I didn't say anything to Jerry, I just stood looking up at the stars, making up my mind. Just then he said:

"Come, what are you gazing up there for? Hurry up; it's getting late."

Just as quick as a wink it came to me, that verse, you know, where the hand pointed, about the men gazing up, and about Jesus coming again. "What if He should come tonight while I'm down at the mill-pond!" I said to myself; and somehow I felt as though I would rather not be at the mill-pond if He did. Just then I laughed right out:

"I won't climb any hedge tonight," says I. "I've got pricked trying."

Jerry he turned and looked at me, and says:

"Are you getting crazy? Who said anything about a hedge? Going to the pond or not?"

"Not," I said and skipped into the house. What do you think? There sat Mother! She missed the six o'clock train and the lightning express which doesn't ever stop here, stopped for her because Major Dennis was on and the President of the road or something. Anyhow, Mother came in from the depot in the express wagon and Hannah had slipped out and got some oysters and we had the nicest kind of a supper, we three; and I sat by Mother, and she gave me two of the biggest oysters in her plate. Wasn't I glad I wasn't at the mill-pond? But wasn't it odd about that hedge fence? There goes the second bell for school.

Your Cousin,

Frank Hudson

# Chapter II.

*In Him was life, and life was the light of men.*
*Neither is there salvation in any other; for there is*
  *none other name under heaven given among*
  *men, whereby we must be saved.*
*If God be for us, who can be against us?*
*Lying lips are an abomination to the Lord.*

*Cooledge, Feb., 18—*

Dear Renie:

There is my hedge fence for you, as good as I can
make it; doesn't look much like the one that Mr. Harris
Browning sent me; that is the cutest kind of a thing!
Strange, isn't it, that he takes the trouble to make them
for me every month? Mother thought he would forget
but he didn't; he isn't one of the forgetting kind. Well,
sir, you never saw anything like that hedge for helping a
fellow out of scrapes! You said I must tell you every
time it did me a good turn. Old fellow, I couldn't begin
to do it! I should have to write a book. Why, there isn't
a day, no, nor an hour in the day, hardly, but that hedge
pops up before me and says: Look out, sir, you'll tumble
over before you know it, if you take another step this
way. I'll tell you what I'll do: the great big scrapes you

shall hear about; and the others will have to keep until you come. Yesterday we had a time of it at school. Did you ever learn the rule for long division? I think it is rightly named, for if it isn't l-o-n-g, I should like to know what was! Our class was to have it word for word; and ever since Jerry Davis was caught peeking, Mr. Masters hasn't let us take our arithmetic to the class at all; so there is no chance to peek. Well, you better believe I had to work over that old rule! It took me until eight o'clock.

If Mother hadn't helped, I don't believe I should ever have learned it in the world. It's odd how different Mothers are from other folks. I asked Father to help me, and he said, "Help you to learn a rule! That's a strange idea! You must just go to work and master it!" But Mother knows how. She came and sat down by me when I was tugging at it, and feeling doleful, and says she:

"How far do you know?"

"I don't know any far at all," I said. "It's all mixed up."

Then she said we would unmix it; and says she: "What is the first line about?"

Well, sir, do you believe I knew! Not a word of it, and I'd been studying for half an hour. Mother made a motion with her finger, like a curve, you know, and asked me what I put at the left of that line, and I said the divisor; and then I said: "Oh, it's about the divisor. Find how many times the divisor goes into the dividend."

"Into all the figures of the dividend I suppose?" she said; and then I laughed, and told her no; into the fewest figures that would take it; and she went through that muddle with me, and asked funny questions, you know, and made a fellow good natured, and made him think what he was about; and in ten minutes after that, I could say every word of it! Father came in, and says he: "Well, Frank, how's the rule?" "I know it, sir," I said; "Mother got it, and I can say it." But that isn't the beginning of the scrape. Jerry Davis has got a printing press for a Christmas present; and he knows how to use it, cause his uncle is a printer.

What did he do yesterday morning but bring to school the cutest little square of paper, not so big as my hand, with every word of the rule printed on it as nice as could be; and he gave every boy in the class a square. I took it because I thought it was cute, and put it in my pocket. Mr. Masters has a way of marching all around the schoolroom while our class is reciting; and when it came time for the rule, he was away over by the map of North America; so what did the fellows do but stand up and read that rule, one after the other, from their pieces of paper.

"Well done!" Mr. Masters said, and I knew he was astonished, because some of them are awful blunderers. I blundered over mine a little, I was so busy thinking about them.

Then we went to the board, and each fellow had an example as long as from here to your house to do. I was right in the midst of mine when Jerry Davis began to whisper:

"Say, Frank, how do you do this?"

"Davis," said Mr. Masters, "go on with your work."

Then Davis said he couldn't; and Mr. Masters told him to follow his rule; but he couldn't do that, for he had put it in his pocket out of sight.

What did Mr. Masters do next but to tell him to repeat the rule. That he couldn't do, not a word of it! Then Tom Burns was called on to repeat, and he couldn't; and Arthur Perkins couldn't. And by that time Mr. Masters knew there was some trick; and he asked every fellow in that class for the rule. He came down and stood right before them, and they couldn't look on their papers, and not a boy had a word to say.

When he got to me, thanks to Mother, I said it off like a rocket. Then he began to ask questions, and I began to tremble in my boots. What was I going to say? If I told the truth, every fellow would be mad at me. I hate rows, and I couldn't bear to think of it; besides, some of the boys are mean when they are mad, and do things to hurt a fellow like everything. Mr. Masters was asking each boy if he had a written copy of the rule anywhere about him, and every fellow of them said, "No, he hadn't." I about made up my mind to say the same, because I hadn't, you know. The thing was printed. What do you suppose popped up just then but a piece of that hedge to stumble over: "Lying lips are an abomination to the Lord."

"It isn't a lie," I said to myself; "the copy isn't written."

But that was a real thin excuse, for of course, we knew what he meant, and, of course, it would be deceiving him; and it didn't make a hole, even, through the hedge. I saw I'd got to jump it, if I went that way. But I felt awful. I told myself that the boys would all be mad and that the snow was hard just now; and ice balls sometimes hurt awfully; and it was kind of hard to have them all against me when I hadn't done anything wrong; and just then up came another piece of the hedge: "If God be for us, who can be against us?" I tell you, Renie, I made up my mind to risk it; and when he got to me with his question, he said:

"Frank, I hope for the exact truth from you; as you are the only one who doesn't seem to depend on a trick to help you through with your lesson. Do you know anything about a written copy of the rule that these boys could have looked at?"

Says I: "I haven't a written copy, but I have a printed one in my pocket."

Well, he called for it, of course, and I had to show it. He asked where I got it, and I asked if he wouldn't excuse me from telling; and he did, and sent us to our seats. But all those fellows had to stay, and there was no end of a time!

And they are mad at me, every one of them; and Jerry Davis says he will teach me a thing or two before the winter is over. But Mother says, suppose they do pitch snowballs at me, I can melt them with coals of fire. It took me a good hour, and a hint from Mother about what the Bible said, before I understood what she could mean. The Bible is an odd book, I think. There's most everything in it. Do you know about the "coals of fire?"

I'm practicing on them. I sent Jerry Davis a book from my Christmas set to read tonight.

Mother says tell Aunt Jane to write. So no more this time.

From your cousin,
Frank Hudson

# Chapter III.

*We ought to obey God rather than men.*
*Seven men of honest report, full of the Holy Ghost*
*and wisdom.*
*Be thou faithful unto death, and I will give thee a*
*crown of life.*

*Cooledge, March, 18—*

Dear Renie:

Now, says I, if I haven't got a strange thing to tell you, then no fellow ever had, that's all. There, I've gone and said "got" again, and I promised Miss Kennedy I wouldn't. There's such an awful lot of things of that kind to remember it's enough to make a boy gray. There I go again! If Miss Kennedy were to see this she would say, "My dear Frank, does that really fill you with awe?" Then I should say, "Yes, ma'am, it does." She won't see this letter, that is one comfort. She is our new teacher, and she is just perfectly splendid. I try awful hard to please her, but she will never know it, for I don't succeed worth a cent.

But about the hedge fence. Well, you see the way of it was that I went home with Tim to stay till Monday. Tim goes to school, you know, and boards here. He goes home Friday nights; it is six miles on the cars. Mother didn't much like my going, but I coaxed, and Father said, "Don't you think the boy is getting old enough to hop out of the nest once in awhile?" So Mother finally agreed that I might go.

Well, my new hedge fence had come just the night before, and I didn't think much of it. The drawing was cuter than ever; just the ugliest kind of little bits of wretches peeking out on the other side of the hedge trying to get hold of me. But the verses didn't seem to have anything in them to help a fellow. I didn't expect to have anything to do with people who would want me to do wrong things, and I knew my reports were always "honest," if they weren't anything else, and it didn't seem to me that I had anything to be faithful about. But I took the card along, kind of wishing all the while that since I was going away from home I had a hedge that would help keep me straight. Much I knew about it.

Tim's mother is nice I s'pose, for him, but I wouldn't like her for mine. There's as much difference in mothers as there is in everything else. We had pretty good times on Saturday, and got awful tired, and they had supper late, and had raw oysters and plum jam, and lots of milk and things, and I guess I ate a good deal.

Well, sir, in the night I was sick, most awful sick. I rolled and tumbled about that bed and cried like a trooper. Tim got up and called his mother, and she said I had bilious colic she guessed, and asked me if I had ever been so before. And I told her I had, and Mother always gave me something that helped me, and what did she say but that she would bring me a little hot brandy and water which would help me right away. I was all doubled up with a pain just then, but I straightened myself out, and says I, "Oh, no, ma'am, I can't take that; Mother never gives it. I'll be better in a little while, I guess."

Then Tim spoke up, and says he, "Why, Frank, it is real good; Mother puts lots of sugar in it. I always take it when I'm sick, and I like it first-rate." Then I told them that I wasn't such a baby that I couldn't swallow medicine whether I liked it or not; but that Mother never used brandy, and she didn't want me to, and I had taken the pledge years ago, never to touch, taste, nor handle the stuff, and meant to keep it. Well, sir, we had just an awful time. That mother she went off and fixed the brandy, and she said she hadn't anything else that would do so much good, and that all people took brandy for medicine; but I told her that Father and Mother never did, and didn't believe in it; and every few minutes that awful pain would come and double me right up; and she said maybe I would die if I was so obstinate as not to take medicine; that folks did sometimes. I didn't think I would die, because I had had that sort of thing before. But I stuck to it that I couldn't take brandy, because I had promised not to. When I took the pledge that time I wrote you about when I was a little fellow, Mother and I prayed about it a good deal, and she had me promise God that with His help I would never taste the stuff. How was I to take brandy and sugar after that? After awhile that mother got angry; she did truly, and she said:

"I never did see such a provoking boy! Mr. Truax, I wish you would come down here and see if you can do anything with him." He's the father. So he came and leaned over the bed and glowered at me, and says he: "Frank, you are here under our care while away from your parents, and that being the case, of course you must obey us. Now I command you to swallow the medicine that Mrs. Truax has brought you. There is reason in all things."

"I can't do it," says I; "I'm hedged in, 'We ought to obey God rather than men;' that is my hedge fence, and I've promised not to try to climb it."

Oh, well; if I were to sit up all night and write, I couldn't tell you the whole story. It was just the meanest time a fellow ever had in his life. By and by the pain was better; but I felt sore all over, and everybody in that house was mad at me. That mother said she didn't believe in children being wiser than their elders, and lots of other hateful things. Then it got to be morning, and they all went off and left me; and I just lay there and cried, and wanted Mother, and thought how was I going to wait till Monday morning, and me so sore and everybody mad. Oh, it was awful! All the same I was glad that I hadn't jumped the hedge; because Mother and Father don't believe in it for medicine, either, and they think that God doesn't. Well, the folks had their breakfast; I didn't want any; and when that mother came and asked me if there was anything that I thought it was right to eat, I just said, "No, ma'am," as quick as I could, and then I turned my face to the wall and cried again.

The clothes were all tumbled up, and it was awful. After awhile I went to sleep and dreamed I was home; and when I felt myself waking up I tried to stay asleep, because I knew I wasn't at home. Then somebody stooped down and kissed me. I opened my eyes in a hurry, and there was Mother. I'll tell you how it was. You see Phil Truax is a young man; his room is next to Tim's, and he opened his door when the row came, and heard it all. So what did he do but get up by and by, and harness his horse and drive all those six miles—but it is only four miles by the road when you drive—after Mother. And he told her all about it. He said there was a young captain in the enemy's camp, and he had made up his mind that the general (that was Mother) ought to come to his aid. Then Mother said he looked sad and said, if he had been hedged in when he was my age, he would never have got lost out in the woods as he is now. He drinks, Phil Truax does, and Mother is very sorry for him; and I'm going to try to coax him to sign my pledge. Mother was glad that I didn't climb the hedge. She made everything straight at Tim's, and they think she is a lady. I know one thing; I don't want to go visiting again in a hurry.

Good-bye,
Frank Hudson

# Chapter IV.

*Thy heart is not right in the sight of God.*
*And he went on his way rejoicing.*
*And he received sight forthwith, and arose, and*
*was baptized.*
*He which persecuted us in times past, now*
*preaches the faith which once he destroyed.*
*Jesus Christ maketh thee whole.*

*Cooledge, April,* 18—

Dear Renie:

We've had the greatest lark out! All kind of mixed up with my hedge fence, too. It's a real long story—almost too long for a letter, I guess, but I'll hurry it up. The folks are well, and nothing has happened to any of 'em, only Katie's had the measles, and Charlie the mumps, so I needn't take time telling you about them.

You see, the other day it was the first of April, and we boys had been planning a joke on Alvin Burke; he's a boy in our school who works for his board down at the factory boarding-house, and we don't know him very well because he never had any time to play, and always seemed kind of glum. He is a great fellow to study, though, and always has his lessons; beats us in spelling, and such things, all to pieces, but he has been away behind in arithmetic; it is because he never had a chance to go to school before. Next week our spring term begins, and Alvin wants to go in our arithmetic; he has been working awful hard, and he thinks he can keep up, and the teacher is willing to have him try it, if he can get an arithmetic. Well, sir, that fellow has sold his broken-bladed knife, and his old rubber ball, and a storybook that somebody gave him, and I don't know but he would have sold his teeth, if he could have had them pulled out, trying to get an arithmetic; it is the advanced kind, and they cost a dollar and a quarter. It seemed so funny to us boys to see him dig in, that we nicknamed him "Rithy"; that's the short, you see, for arithmetic; and about a week before April fool, we got up a notion. At Freehold's store they have odd little tin boxes to look exactly like a book, red edges and all, and I noticed that they were just the size of our arithmetics so I told the boys, and we agreed that it would be a jolly lark to buy one of those boxes, and get Jerry Davis to letter it, and wrap it up in paper, and send it to Alvin; he'd be sure to think it was a real book.

The boys all went into it, and thought it was rich. Charlie Porter said it was nicer than most April fools, for it was a real nice box to keep pencils and things in, and Alvin might be glad to get it; it only cost a quarter. We put our money together, and bought it, and had the letters put on with Jerry Davis' printing press, and you never saw a cuter thing.

## A Hedge Fence

We were going to lay it on Alvin's desk Monday morning, and have the fun of seeing him open it. Well, I carried it home to take care of, that evening, and on the way I stopped at the post-office, and there was my hedge fence. Just a beauty it was, all fixed up with green ink, and the verses peeking out at me.

I don't know what made me keep reading over the first one so much: I never noticed the others at all. That one kind of seemed to stick me, and says I to myself, "It kind of seems as though I must be trying to climb that hedge, for I feel a thorn."

By and by I began to talk out loud. Says I, "Why, I'm sure there's nothing mean about that—just a little fun; he gets a nice tin box. If he is a little disappointed, he isn't a baby."

But the more I thought, the worse I felt; something kept saying to me, "You know you are not doing it because you want Alvin to have a nice tin box; you want to see how hot his face will get, and how his great gray eyes will look first glad and then sullen, and you boys all want to giggle and whisper, 'April fool!' It doesn't look very mean on the outside, but down in your heart, old fellow, I shouldn't wonder if you were ashamed of it." Well, if you'll believe it, I got so scratched every time I tried the hedge, that at last I went straight to Mother and we had a talk, and I had a plan, and she agreed to it, and I went out after supper, and asked all the five boys to come and eat apples in our dining-room for an hour. They all came, and when I had a chance, says I, "Boys, let's make a clean thing of it, and put the arithmetic

inside; see how it fits!" and I popped my old book into
the box, and it was a perfect fit.

They looked astonished, and they all wanted to talk
at once and asked what was the matter, and all that; and
I squirmed around it awhile, and then I up and told them
about the hedge fence, and the thorn that was scratching
into me. They laughed some, but pretty soon Charlie
Porter began to rub his leg, and says he, "Boys, I believe
I'm scratched, too; let's tumble back and fall in with
Frank; I've got a quarter saved up from Christmas, that
I'll give." And if you'll believe it, every boy of the five
agreed to it! Some of them hadn't any money, but
Mother came in and talked the thing over, as nice as
though she had been a boy herself, and she said she
would advance the money, and open an account with
them, and they agreed to earn it, and if their fathers were
willing, they would all do it. And the next morning the
fathers were willing, and we all went to the bookstore
and bought as nice an arithmetic as the man had, and he
threw off a quarter, so it only cost us twenty cents apiece.

But the funniest part of the lark is to come. We
carried it to Alvin's desk, all tied up in white paper, and
do you believe he wouldn't open it! He thought it was a
piece of board, done up like a book. We watched him all
the morning, and he shoved the thing around with his
elbow, tossing his head, and looking awful fierce, and
pretty soon he slammed it down on the floor.

We got around him at noon, and coaxed him to let us
see it. "Do you suppose I'm a fool?" he asked us. "It's

nothing but a board wrapped up, and I know where it came from, too."

Charlie Porter told him he didn't believe it was a board, it didn't look like one, and says he: "See here, Alvin, if it is a board I'll give you twenty cents for it. I will, as sure as my name is Charlie Porter." So Alvin opened it, and I just wish you could have seen his face! First he thought it was an arithmetic, the box was, you know, and then he found it wasn't, and he was awfully disappointed, and he tried not to show it; and then he found there was an arithmetic inside, with his name in it, and it said under the name: "From Some April Fools." Well, sir, he just jumped up and down and shouted! It was the jolliest time!

Mother says I must go to bed this minute, so good-by.

    From,
        Frank Hudson

# Chapter V.

*On the Gentiles also was poured out the gift of the
Holy Ghost.*
*And the hand of the Lord was with them; and a
great number believed, and turned unto the
Lord.*
*The angel of the Lord encampeth round about
them that fear him, and delivereth them.*
*Separate me, Barnabas and Saul, for the work
whereunto I have called them.*

*Cooledge, May,* 18—

Dear Renie:

Father says he believes in hedge fences. He thinks
he has good reason too. I'll tell you about it. I carried
this one to Mother as soon as it came. That is, it came
Saturday night, and I showed it to Mother on Sunday.
She and I were having a little talk. I told her there wasn't
a thing in it this time that could help me; that there was
nothing to make a hedge of.

But she didn't agree with me. She said she thought
they were all good for hedges, but that last verse was a
grand one. Now the last verse was the one that I was the
most sure couldn't do me any good. I told her I didn't

see how; that every single one of the verses was about other people; the sort of verses, you know, that a fellow couldn't twist to make belong to himself; and the last one was miles away.

Then Mother said: "Why, Frank, I am astonished! Haven't you been separated by the same One Who called them? And hasn't He a particular work for you to do?"

Then I knew that Mother meant about my coming to Christ, which I did two Sundays ago, you know I told you. But I had never thought about having any work to do; not that He picked out for me. Well, we talked it over, Mother and I. She said she knew He would show me my work when I was ready to do it, and that she hoped I would remember that I was separated from the folks who didn't love Him, and must not go anywhere to soil my clothes. She laughed when I looked puzzled, and said she was thinking of the time when I was a little fellow and she used to get me ready for church. Tim was here then, and he used to coax me to come out in the garden, but I would shake my head and say: "I can't; I'm all Sunday now, and must sit still."

There was more talk that I haven't time to tell you about, but I thought of it ever so many times that day.

The next afternoon the Smith boys and that Nickerson fellow that I never have much to do with, were out in front of our yard playing marbles. They asked me to come and play, and I went a few minutes; but Sam Smith had bad luck and at last began to swear.

Pretty soon Joe Nickerson answered him in the same way. Now I often have to hear that kind of talk, and I had always thought that if I kept still it was the most I could do; but right off there popped into my head that verse about being "separated." Said I to myself, "I'm not separated much, now that's a fact, so long as I stay here and roll marbles. A body who did not know me, might think I would swear too, whenever I felt like it."

I waited a little, but the swearing kept on and I made up my mind to "separate" myself. "Boys," says I, "I'll have to leave." Then they began to coax me not to go, and Sam Smith said he had a nice plan; his mother told him he might bring half a dozen boys home to supper, because it was his birthday, and he asked me to be one of them. But I said I would have to go in, and when they got at me for a reason, I thought I ought to tell them, or else it would not be separating myself. So I up and told them that I had made up my mind not to stay any more where folks swore. Then they got mad. They called me "Parson Hudson" and they said since I had joined the church, I thought I was too good for common folks, and that I ought to be tied to my mother's apron string for fear I should hear somebody say something that wasn't pretty. Then they began to swear again, all three of them, and I ran into the house: and they hooted at me. I told Mother about it; I said I had separated myself as well as I knew how, but I didn't see as there was any chance in it to work. But she told me not to try to go too fast.

It wasn't till the next morning that I heard the rest of the story. Don't you believe Sam's mother had not told him he might ask any of the boys to tea, but he did, and he thought she would be sure to give them some supper when they got there. Instead, she sent them all home. Wouldn't I have enjoyed it to be one of them.

Well, they were mad about it, and they made up their minds to have some fun: so they went to Widow Hurlburt's garden and tramped down the plants and did lots of mischief, and let the pig into the vegetable garden and spoiled everything. There were five of them; and they got found out and taken up, and the widow was willing to settle it if the fathers would pay five dollars apiece for each boy. They say that one boy didn't do a thing, only looked on, but his father had to pay, all the same. When Father told Mother and me about it, Mother said: "Frank, my boy, you see one good result from separating yourself, don't you?" And she told father all about it, and he said that a hedge fence that saved him five dollars in one night, was worth thinking about.

But I told Mother that, after all, I didn't see any work for me to do, and she said, wait, that I hadn't heard the end of the story yet, perhaps; that there was no telling what I might do, some time, for those very boys, because they would keep watch of me now, to see if I was to be trusted in other things. Then after a minute she said softly, "You don't know how large a work you may have begun in interesting your father in your hedge fence."

I thought about that a good deal, and I made up my mind I would ask you to help me pray for Father. He is real splendid good, you know, only he isn't a Christian, and Mother and I want him to be dreadfully.

Your cousin,
Frank Hudson

# Chapter VI.

*And the Word of the Lord was published*
*throughout all the region.*
*Speaking boldly in the Lord.*
*Go ye therefore and teach all nations, baptizing*
*them in the name of the Father, and of the Son,*
*and of the Holy Ghost.*

*Cooledge, June* 18—

Dear Renie:

There's lots to tell you this time: all the folks around here have been having the mumps: some of them look too funny for anything. Their cheeks puff out, you know, and their noses look twisted, and they can't eat, nor laugh, nor anything.

Jimmy Tucker had them, and I went to see him at noon, and took him a pickle that was left from my lunch; you ought to have heard him yell! It seems that the mumps don't like pickles. I didn't know it. I was awfully sorry for Jimmy, and yet to save my life I couldn't help laughing.

There! I've gone and told another story. Mother says that whenever I say I couldn't stop doing some silly little thing *to save my life*, I am telling what isn't true;

that if it would have saved my life to stop laughing at Jimmy Tucker, I could have done it in a twinkling. I s'pose I could, but it is an awful lot of trouble to be so particular all the time about what you say. Well, it was because of the mumps that I went on a journey. You see our school got so full of them that there was no room for studying, and we had to close for a week. That was the way Mother came to take me with her to Orange, N. J., for a little visit.

We started real early in the morning, and I had to bring my things the night before to pack in Mother's trunk. I brought my best necktie, and my gold cuff buttons, and my new hair brush, and then Mother called after me, and said, "Frank, don't forget your hedge fence!"

I had to stop in the door and laugh; it seemed so funny to hear a fellow told to bring a *hedge fence* to pack in a trunk.

"I guess I'll carry that in my pocket," I told her at last, when I got through laughing, "but there won't be a bit of use for it this time. It is all about preaching. It doesn't hedge me up a bit. I can't be expected to stand up in a pulpit and preach."

"Humph!" Mother said, "because you can't stand up in a pulpit and do it, you have nothing to say about the Lord! That's an odd idea. Then His word won't be published through Orange by any help of yours, eh?"

Well, sir, I went off feeling kind of strange. It was a new notion to me that I had got to do anything about *publishing things*. I told Mother that that was not what the fence was for; it was to hedge me in when I was going to do anything wrong. She didn't answer that, only just looked at me and smiled.

What do you think? I hadn't been in Orange but one day, before a boy where Mother and I visited, asked me to go to a P. S. Club.

They were just going to organize, and they meant to meet once a month, and have talking and singing, and stories told, and oh! lots of nice things. I went, and it was real pleasant. Pretty soon, after they had elected their President and other officers, they began to plan how to open their meeting. Some of them said it ought to be done with singing, and some said that reading the report of the last meeting was a good enough way to open. Well, I know all about the P. S., and their whisper motto is,

For Jesus' Sake,

and I thought the way to open would be to pray a few words; but I had no notion of saying such a thing, until up popped that fence of mine about "speaking boldly in the Lord." Do you believe I could get away from the notion that I ought to tell those boys and girls what I thought? Pretty soon they up and asked me what my opinion was. Then, says I, it was a clear case: either I had got to jump that hedge fence out and out, and sneak behind it, or else I must speak out boldly. It was real hard work, but I said that it was none of my business, seeing I didn't belong, but *I* should think that a society with such a whisper motto as theirs, ought to begin with prayer. You ought to have heard how still they kept for a minute; it was just awful!

Then Bert Holland, a little fellow, said an odd thing. "Boys don't pray," said he. He seemed scared to think he had spoken, and his face got red. It sounded so strange that we all laughed. Then Harry Bolton, a real splendid boy, spoke out boldly, I tell you.

"Some boys do," said he, "and I think Frank Hudson is right. I move that we begin our meetings with prayer."

They put it to vote and it carried, and then the hardest part of it came: what did they do but ask me to pray, right then and there! It was awful hard work, but I stood up and said, "God bless all these girls, and boys, for Jesus' sake. Amen."

We had a real splendid good time, and the boys were all nice to me, and hoped I would come again, and I wish I could.

I meant to tell you all about Orange, and how I went to New York while I was there, and rode on the elevated railway and crossed back and forth on a ferry, and went to Central Park, but there isn't room this time; I must write a letter on purpose.

When we were riding home, while the cars were rattling with all their might, Mother leaned over to me, and said:

"Frank, seems to me you have found a way to preach a little, without going into a pulpit. Mrs. West told me her boy decided that evening of the P.S. meeting to do things heartily for Jesus' sake. She thinks your words helped him."

I told her it was all because of the hedge, that I couldn't jump it. But I do think that mothers have such nice sweet ways of saying things to a fellow.

Good-by,

Frank Hudson

# Chapter VII.

*Be strong in the Lord, and in the power of His might.*
*When thou passest through the waters, I will be with thee; and through the rivers, they shall not overthrow thee.*
*By faith the walls of Jericho fell down, after they were compassed about seven days.*
*Be sure your sin will find you out.*
*I have set before you life and death, blessing and cursing.*

*Cooledge, July* 18—

Dear Renie:

Now what will you say, I wonder? Don't you believe I have gone and jumped that hedge fence after all?

Maybe you are not a bit surprised, but I must say that I am; because you see, I had got so kind of used to being helped by it, that I thought I would keep on the right side of it, of course.

This is the way it was: Fourth of July is coming, you know, and we boys were all getting ready for it.

Every fellow but me was buying lots of fire crackers; and a good many of them bought powder. They got their things so long beforehand, because they were afraid they wouldn't have any money left when the day came, and besides it is kind of nice to be all ready.

Well, you know Mother, and how she feels about powder and things; she grows worse and worse. Since that accident last Fourth of July with the toy cannon, she turns pale when anybody says powder before her. I don't wonder much. But now, honestly, doesn't it seem a little speck odd to be afraid of fire crackers? Not that I want any; I hate the sight of the sneaking red things.

But I was going to tell you about it.

Of course we promised, Tim and I, three years ago, that we wouldn't buy any, nor fire any; but this year—

Why, you see it's this way: the boys around here are apt to make fun of you if you don't buy firecrackers. And one day when the Smith boys and Joe Nickerson were saying some pretty mean things, like "Does your mother allow you to sneeze when you feel like it?" and "Do you have to ask her when you want to wink your eye?" and all that silliness, it made me feel awful! Just as though they were making fun of Mother, you know; and thinks I to myself, I'll show them a thing or two. I had a whole quarter of a dollar in my pocket, and what did I do but go in with the boys and spend every cent of it in firecrackers! I had my hedge fence in my pocket, too; but if you'll believe it, I didn't see a thing in that hedge about firecrackers, until I had bought them.

Then what did it do but begin to prick me. "Be sure your sin will find you out." That is what it kept whispering to me over and over, until I really got mad.

"I haven't done any sin," I told it, "and there's nothing to find out. I'm sure I didn't do anything in secret; all the fellows saw me."

"Yes; but your mother didn't, and you know she told you not to buy any."

"That was three years ago," said I, "she hasn't said firecrackers to me this summer."

"That's because she trusts you."

"Well, she can trust me now; I'm not going to fire a cracker of them; I mean to give them to some boy whose mother doesn't care."

"But you know you are not going to tell your mother a thing about it."

"Well, what if I'm not? That is only so she won't be worried."

Did you ever argue with a thing in your pocket? It is the strangest how it will keep on and on, after you think there isn't anything more to say? Why, I believe it said that verse over to me twenty times on the way home!

Well, I had the dreadfullest time with those crackers! I couldn't think who to give them to; you see I hadn't thought, when I bought them, of giving them away. I just wanted to show the fellows that I wasn't afraid to buy firecrackers. I couldn't find a place to put the things. First I tucked them into my drawer, away down among the stockings; and then I remembered that the next day was Friday, and that Mother would be in there to regulate my drawer and see that everything was straight; so then I put them in my new boots that I don't wear, only Sundays; and in less than an hour afterwards what should I hear but Father calling out to Mother to have Frank's boots sent down to him and he would see about those pegs that hurt! I tore up the stairs in a hurry, before Mother could step from her room into mine, and whipped those firecrackers under the bed.

But I knew that wouldn't do, for Friday is sweeping day, too. At last I made up my mind to dig a little hole in the back yard and bury them. So I went at it. And I tell you I had no end of a time.

There wasn't a boarder in the house that didn't want me to do something for them, between the time that I went at that job and the time when I got it done! Mother called me twice, and I had to hide the stupid things in my hat and run bareheaded. And Mother said: "Frank, don't work out in the hot sun without your hat. Run and get it. What are you doing?"

"Planting," says I, and I had to scud, before she could ask me what I was planting.

At last they were hid in the ground; but all the time that creature in my pocket kept saying: "Be sure your sin will find you out." I·was so provoked at it, that I had a mind to dig another hole and bury it.

Well, sir, I made up my mind not to give the firecrackers away, but to let them lie in the ground where they would keep still and do no harm. But I didn't count on Fluff nor Snip. Fluff has ten chickens and goes clucking and scratching around for them all the time.

Day before yesterday she slipped into the garden, and just as I got home from school and was resting me a minute on Mother's lounge, and telling Father that I was at the head of the History class, who should come in wagging his tail but Snip, and what did he have in his mouth but that long bunch of firecrackers that I thought were safely buried.

"Dear me!" said Mother, "where did Snip get these?" And something said to me, didn't I tell you that your sin would find you out?

We've got a new girl and her name is Maria; she came in, just then, and told Father that Fluff had slipped into the garden and scratched up the corn, and that string of firecrackers! Father ran to see to Fluff, and I thought that Mother stayed to see to me. But she only sewed away on my new shirt, and said she:

"Some of the boys must be trying to play a joke on Frank; they are not his, Maria, for he never buys any, nor handles any, because his mother does not like them."

Now wasn't that hard on a fellow! She looked over at me when she said it and smiled the nicest smile there ever was on a mother's face. There I was with my sin finding me out sure enough. I knew now that it was a great big sin from beginning to end, and nothing else, and Mother hadn't found it out because she trusted me!

It was awful! If there had not been another verse in my hedge fence I don't know what I should have done. Did you notice that first one? "Be strong in the Lord and in the power of His might."

That came into my mind just then, and said I to myself: "I will." I went over to Mother, and sat down on the stool in front of her, and I told the whole story about those firecrackers from beginning to end.

Well, sir, she was just as good as gold. I know she felt bad, for her cheeks got red, and once she said: "Oh, Frank!" but I went on fast, and told about it, and about the hedge fence, and all, and said I was sorrier than she could think. She hunted up a boy whose mother washes here sometimes, and she told Mother that she would like to get him some firecrackers, but she couldn't afford the money; and I went and took the things to him, and he was as glad as he could be, and so was I. And I'll tell you what it is, I mean to try to be "strong in the Lord" beforehand, instead of afterward.

Mother says that perhaps when I am twenty-one she will get over her fear of firecrackers and agree to my firing them; but I told her she needn't hurry, for I believed I should hate the things until I was eighty-one at least.

I didn't mean to write such a long letter; but it was a long story, you see.

    Good-by,

      Frank Hudson

# Chapter VIII.

*Who have fled for refuge to lay hold on the hope*
*set before us.*
*Choose you this day whom ye will serve.*
*And they forsook the Lord God of their fathers.*
*The sword of the Lord, and of Gideon.*

*Cooledge, August* 18—

Dear Renie:

I will tell you what it is, that hedge fence of mine is just the nicest thing a fellow ever had. It is big enough to reach around other folks, don't you think!

It is a long story, and a real splendid one.

It began in this way: Mother and I stood at the window one night last week, just before dark, looking at the hedge fence. It had just come in a paste-board box. It is prettier this month than ever; it has a lovely wreath of forget-me nots all around the border.

Mother was just reading the third verse when Rene Marshall went by. You are his namesake, you know, and he is real nice. I've always liked him, because he is good-natured to us boys. Mother sighed when she saw him, and said, "There is one who is doing it, Frank."

"Doing what, ma'am?" I said, and I looked out of the window after Rene.

"Doing that verse; whenever I see him, I feel afraid that he is getting farther away from the God of his fathers. He had a splendid father. One of the greatest temperance men we ever had in Cooledge. I have heard him plead with old Joe Bates until I couldn't keep the tears out of my eyes: and think what a good man Joe is now! And poor Rene, with a good father gone to heaven, is going downhill."

"But, Mother!" I said, "Rene isn't a drunkard!"

"No," Mother said, "he isn't yet; but I tremble for him. His father signed the temperance pledge when he was younger than you are, and never touched, tasted, nor handled; and Rene, they tell me, takes wine at their parties, and cider all the time. Such things almost always end badly."

It made me feel just awful to think that Mother thought Rene could ever go staggering through the streets a drunkard!

It was the very next afternoon that I stood on the post-office steps waiting for the mail, when Rene came to the door of the ice-cream saloon, and says he:

"Come here, Frank, and get a taste of raspberry wine; it is refreshing."

Says I, "No sir; not I, thank you. I can't be jumping a hedge for the sake of some raspberry wine."

Rene looked puzzled a minute, and then he laughed, and asked if the heat had taken away my senses.

"It isn't intoxicating," he said, holding up his glass and looking through it.

"It has alcohol in it," I told him; "Father said all those things that sparkled so, and tasted bright and snappy, were beginning to make alcohol. And I don't want to begin his acquaintance. Father feels so, and Grandfather did, and his great grandfather did, and I'm hedged up, and I don't mean to jump. Look here!"

Then I out with my hedge fence and showed him the verse: They forsook the Lord God of their fathers. "I don't want to have that said of me," I told Rene. Then I said: "What makes you forsake it, Rene? Mother told me the other night about your father, what a good man he was, and a temperance man and all. I should think you would want him to hedge you up."

After I had said it I was scared, Rene looked at me so strangely! He didn't say a word. Just turned and went back into the saloon, and it wasn't until after he had gone that I remembered he had taken my hedge fence with him.

I didn't like to go in and ask for it, so I went without it all the week. I didn't see a sight of Rene until Sunday night: then I went to the young folks' prayer meeting, and who should get up but Rene Marshall! I never saw him there before, and it was so still you could have heard a pin drop when he began to speak. I can tell you every word he said:

"My friends, I have been walking on very dangerous ground, and my feet have well-nigh slipped, but I have been "hedged in"; my father's God has sought me and set a wall about me. I trust that I am saved."

Well, sir, if Dick Woods hadn't at just that minute begun to sing:

Hallelujah 'tis done, I believe on the Son,

I guess I would have yelled. I did yell that hymn out as loud as I could. I think hallelujah is a splendid word to sing.

Isn't that nice? Rene is grand, now. I told Father that he had helped to save Rene Marshall. He didn't understand, and I had to tell him about the hedge fence, and how I told Rene that I was following my father, in not touching alcohol, or any of his relations.

Then Mother said something low to him which I didn't understand. It was about "healing himself," though what she meant, I'm sure I don't know.

Mother is calling me to come and help pick blackberries for tea, and this must call itself done.

Good-by,

Frank Hudson

# Chapter IX.

*The God of Israel is he that giveth strength and*
*    power unto his people.*
*Thy people shall be my people, and thy God my*
*    God.*
*I have lent him to the Lord: as long as he liveth he*
*    shall be lent to the Lord.*
*Speak, Lord, for thy servant heareth.*

Cooledge, Sep. 18—

Dear Renie:

We've had our picnic. We went up to Beldon's
woods, us boys, you know, and a lot of the girls; we had
a real jolly time. They had fried potatoes for supper, and
you never saw the way the folks kept calling for them.
It's odd how the woods makes things taste; but as true as
you live, they were better than cake!

Mother broiled three chickens for me to take, and
every boy and girl there wanted a piece, because they
said Mother cooked chickens nicer than anybody else.

I always knew she did, but it seems odd to me that
other folks didn't think just so about their Mothers. I
told Mr. Barnes that, and he said if I lived long enough I
would find that there was a difference in boys as well as

in mothers: though what that had to do with the subject, is more than I know.

But I wasn't going to tell you about that. It is the swimming story that I am to write about.

You see there is a lake up there, and a lot of us planned to go in swimming. We planned not to say a word to our mothers, because mothers are such fidgety creatures; and I thought mine would be happier if she didn't know anything about it, though there isn't a speck of danger.

Well, about an hour before supper we went off by ourselves, for the swim. We were all sitting on a log waiting for Joe Stevens. He is the best swimmer, and he knows just where to go in, and come out, and all, and we agreed to keep with him. He went back after Charlie Porter and we were to wait on the log till they came.

While we sat there, Dick Burns and two other fellows got to disputing about a little dog. Stephen Jenkins wanted to borrow Dick's for a few days to see if it would teach his some tricks, and Dick wouldn't let him have it.

"It isn't my dog," he kept saying, "I have lent the dog to Charlie Porter to take home with him and keep all winter, and because I am taking care of it for him till he goes home, it is no sign that I have a right to let other folks take it."

"Yes, he is yours," Stephen said; "likely because you have lent him to somebody that you haven't a right to do what you please with him!"

"Ho!" said Dick, "you would be a nice fellow to borrow from. Suppose you should lend me your history to keep for a week, and tomorrow morning Frank, here, should come to me and say, 'I want Stephen Jenkins' history: he said I might have it. He says it is his own, and he has a right to do what he likes with it, and he doesn't care if he did lend it to you."

We all laughed at that, but Stephen said it wasn't the same thing. That the dog hadn't gone away yet, and while it was there, Dick had a right to do as he pleased with it.

"No sir" said Dick. "I'm just keeping the dog for Charlie: he pays for his feed, and takes care of him, and I've signed a paper that he is to belong to Charlie until next spring, and I say I've no more right to lend the dog, then I would have if he had gone over to the hotel where Charlie boards. Have I, boys?"

They all agreed that he hadn't, only me, I didn't say a word. As quick as a flash I saw an old hedge start up to keep me out of that swim. When Mother looked at the hedge for this month, she pointed to the third verse, and said she: "Frank, my boy, that is what I have done with you. Remember that you are His servant, lent as long as you live."

Now it was only a few minutes before this, that I had got kind of cross at myself, wondering whether I ought to go in swimming; and I muttered: "I guess my body is my own: I have a right to swim with it if I want to!" And here it wasn't my own at all.

Then up popped that other hedge: "Speak, Lord, for thy servant heareth."

Was it any ways likely that He had something to say to me about swimming?

If you'll believe it, He had: and just then He seemed to speak. "Honor thy father and thy mother"; those were the very words He said.

Mother hadn't said I mustn't go in swimming. She had not said a word about it: I don't believe she knew there was a lake up there. But if I had asked her, she would have said no quicker than a flash, for she is dreadfully afraid of water.

You see it wasn't exactly *disobeying*, but it was a good way off from the "honoring." Any fellow could see that.

The boys went on talking about the dog, and I went on thinking, and whittling slabs off the log, until the others came up.

"Come," said Joe, "step spry, boys, we'll just have time for a good swim before supper."

Then I hopped up. "Good-by boys," said I, "I'm going to tramp back to camp."

They all began to shout and question, and at last I said to Joe, "I can't go. I've lent my feet, and their Master says it isn't quite the thing to take them in swimming, so they must stay out."

"Are you cracked?" Joe asked.

But Charlie Porter began to whistle. He's quick to understand things, Charlie is.

I went off. I told them I couldn't explain any further, it was a riddle for them to guess.

Well, sir, if you'll believe it, before I got back to the rest, I heard somebody hallooing after me, and I waited, and that was Charlie Porter.

"Was it your mother, Frank?" he asked, and laughed; then he said he was in the same boat, that his mother wouldn't be happy if she knew he was in the water, and he had decided to go back.

The fellows went in swimming, and had a good time, and none of them got drowned, or anything, and nothing bad happened, and they chaffed us a good deal about being afraid. But somehow, I didn't care. I never had a nicer picnic in my life. I could have sung and danced all the time, I felt so nice and happy.

After all the others were tired out, and rather cross, I felt bright and kind of chuckly inside.

Hedges are bothersome, sometimes, but you do have good fun inside of them, I think.

I told Mother all about it, and after the light was out, and she was just going away, she stooped down and kissed me, and said she felt so safe, and glad, and happy.

Mothers' kisses are nice. I just as soon live inside of a hedge as not. But isn't it odd how they bring a fellow all up standing, after he thinks he has things all fixed?

Good-by,
Frank Hudson

# Chapter X.

*His sons made themselves vile, and he restraineth*
*them not.*
*Hitherto hath the Lord helped us.*
*It is better to trust in the Lord, than to put*
*confidence in princes.*
*And all the people shouted, and said: God save the*
*king!*

*Cooledge, Oct.* 18—

Dear Renie:

—Such a time! What do you think—I've been to
New York again! This time with Father. He didn't mean
to take me, and I didn't coax, but at the last minute he
thought he would.

Lots of things happened. I don't know when I shall
tell you about them all. The thing I am going to tell now,
is how I got lost. Yes, sir, right in the streets; and it is
enough sight worse than getting lost in the woods, I can
tell you!

We were going along, Father and I, as fast as we
could rush, and that wasn't very fast, for there was an
awful crowd of people going both ways.

Father had a satchel, and a paper bundle, a great big one, and an umbrella, and two coats to carry, and I had a box of things he was going to take back to the store; and we couldn't keep side by side, the crowd was so great.

Father went ahead, and he kept looking back to say: "You keep close to me, and we'll push through to the street-car."

I kept as close as I could, and the crowd grew larger every minute.

Pretty soon there came along a man with the oddest-looking monkeys you ever saw! They were dressed up, just like men; coats, you know, and collars on, and tall hats, and they were taking off their hats, and bowing, right and left. I never saw anything so funny in my life! I looked after the man, as far as I could see him, but I kept moving along all the time, and when the man got out of sight, I looked for Father, and he was nowhere to be seen! Where he disappeared to is more than I understand to this day. It was just as though he went out of the world. One minute there and the next gone.

I kept hurrying along for quite a little way, because I didn't know what else to do; and I thought maybe some of the crowd hid him from sight and I should see him in a minute.

But I didn't. After awhile I turned around and tried to go back, but there were so many people coming from that way, that I couldn't seem to get along.

Then I saw there was a street at the left, and I thought maybe Father had turned there, so I turned too, but no Father was to be seen and at last I began to understand that I was lost, and I didn't know what to do.

All the people were hurrying along, kind of wildly, and I tried to hurry too, but I couldn't, for now I had nowhere to go.

I began to try to plan what I ought to do. Father was on his way to the hotel; I knew that, but I didn't know what one, and even if I did, how was I to find it? He meant to take a street-car, but I didn't know what car, and I hadn't a single cent of money.

I began to fumble in my pocket to see if I couldn't find something to help me, though I knew just as well as could be that there was no money there. I gave my pocketbook to Father when I was on the cars, because I had heard a good deal about pickpockets, and since I hadn't but seventy cents in the world, I didn't care about being robbed of it.

The only thing there was in my pockets besides my handkerchief, and a few strings, and a ball of twine and some such things, was my hedge fence.

I couldn't think what it was at first, and I pulled it out and looked at it.

"Humph!" says I to myself; "I'm hedged up now in a different fashion. I'm lost, and there's no way to climb out that I can see, and you can't help me. There isn't a thing in this hedge to help a fellow who is lost."

It is the prettiest card that he ever sent me. There is a lovely vine climbing all over the hedge, and on that vine was the verse: "Hitherto hath the Lord helped us."

The letters are made of the roses on the vine, you know. Someway you can't help seeing that verse the first thing.

I said it over, and all at once it seemed to come to me, how many times I had been helped by these hedges.

"It is true," said I to myself; "Hitherto He has helped me, and I suppose He knows I am lost, and don't know what to do. I don't suppose this is any harder to Him than lots of other scrapes that I have got into. Why don't I ask Him to help me now?"

Well, sir, I made up my mind that I would. There didn't seem to be any use in hurrying along and not getting anywhere, and I just thought I would stand still, and ask Him what to do next. I thought I would go up on the steps of a building, because it would look better to stand there. So I stepped to the door of one building, but I saw it was some kind of a saloon—there were bottles and jars, and all sorts of liquor. I made up my mind not to stand there, for I don't like to hang around saloons, so I went on to the next building. This was on a corner, and people were rushing by it from all directions.

I just took my stand, and leaned against the door to keep me from getting jostled over, and then I began to say: "Lord, help me again, for Jesus' sake." Not aloud, you know, but inside.

It was all I could think of to say, and it was just what I wanted, so I thought it would do as well as anything.

One man looked at me pretty hard, and said he:

"What are you doing here, youngster?"

I didn't like the looks of him much, and didn't want to tell him I was lost; so I said I was waiting for my father, and he let me alone.

Well, now you listen, for I've something odd to tell you.

There I stood, and I guess I prayed that prayer over ten thousand times, and I didn't see any way out of it, nor know, what to do, more than a baby would.

And somebody laid his hand on my shoulder, and said: "Why, Frank Hudson, where in the world did you come from?" And that, sir, was Mr. Harris Browning!

Now, how did he happen to be passing that corner just then, and catch a glimpse of me in all that crowd? If I had stood on the steps of the saloon, he wouldn't have seen me. Almost the first words he said after he found me out, about things, were, "Now I see a reason for missing the car I wanted. I thought it was very important for me to catch it, but, instead, it seems I was to come down to this corner and catch you."

After that, I knew I wasn't lost any more, but Father didn't know it, and I felt bad for him.

I told Mr. Browning about it, hedge fence and all. He asked a good many questions as to where Father intended to go and when he found I knew nothing about it he said: "Well, Frank, my boy, hold on to your Helper: you can't do better. He will show us the way out. We'll do the best we can, and trust Him for the rest. What is this great bundle you are carrying?"

Then I told him that it was to go back to the store, and that it was to have been there before ten o'clock the next morning, and that I ought to find Father before that time, or I was afraid it would make trouble.

"Suppose we take it back," said he, "then that will be so much done. Do you understand what was to be said?"

Yes, I understood all about that, for I had heard Father and Mother talk; and the address of the store was on the box, so he said we would just take a car and go there at once.

And we did. It was an awful long way. But we did the business all nice, and then we left a message for Father that I was in Mr. Browning's care and would be found at his boarding-house. But I didn't think Father would call there, until he found me, and it seemed dreadful to think of his flying over the city hunting for me.

While Mr. Browning was talking, and writing his address, I just went to praying again, as hard as I could pitch in. It wasn't for myself this time, but for Father; and what do you think I heard while I stood there in that door saying over, "O Lord, help us again," but my own father's voice; he was saying to a policeman:

"I'm in great trouble. I've lost my boy."

I shouted right out: "No, you haven't, Father; here I am."

Well, I sha'n't try to tell you the rest. Father cried and I cried, and we had a great time.

But this is what I want to know:

How came Mr. Harris Browning to walk down that street, instead of some other, and how came Father to come up to that policeman, a mile away from where he left me, and speak so that I could hear him? I don't know, but doesn't it look as though somebody planned it who knew how?

I asked Mr. Browning why he thought God had me get lost in the first place, and he said he should think God didn't do that, it was the monkeys, and my turning my head the wrong way, instead of keeping my eyes on Father all the time, but God helped me out of my trouble.

Good-bye,

Frank Hudson

## Are you looking

for exceptional Christ-honoring, character-building classics for your children? Do you want to make the Bible real to your children? The *Golden Text* series is a wonderful start.

Other available *Golden Text* titles by Isabella Alden are:

| | |
|---|---|
| *The Browning Boys* | *The Exact Truth* |
| *A Dozen of Them* | *We Twelve Girls* |
| *Side by Side* | *Six O'clock in the Evening* |

Other fine titles by Mrs. Alden include the *Ester Ried* series, the *Chautauqua* series, the *Randolph* series, and many other superb individual titles. We also have available quite a number of outstanding reprints by genuine Christian authors like Walton, Havergal, Ropes and others.

Check out our first-class, hand-picked curriculum materials, resources, projects and miscellaneous "growing tools" for young people, and useful materials for the family as a whole. These can all be found in our catalog, *Good Things for Your Family*, available free. Just write, call or visit our web site.

Keepers of the Faith, Co.
PO Box 100
Ironwood, MI 49938-0100
906 663 6881
www.keepersofthefaith.com

Orders shipped within 24 hrs.